SHOWING
SILVER

Copyright © 2025 by Evelyn Linwood

All rights reserved.

No part of this book may be reproduced in any form or by any electronic or mechanical means, including information storage and retrieval systems, without written permission from the author, except for the use of brief quotations in a book review.

Without in any way limiting the author's and publisher's exclusive rights under copyright, any use of this publication to "train" generative artificial intelligence (AI) technologies to generate text is expressly prohibited. The author reserves all rights to license uses of this work for generative AI training and development of machine learning language models.

The story, all names, characters, and incidents portrayed in this production are fictitious. No identification with actual persons (living or deceased), places, buildings, and products is intended or should be inferred.

ISBN: 979-8-9927388-0-3 (ebook)

ISBN: 979-8-9927388-1-0 (print)

Book Cover by Yosbe Design

Map by William Bauer

First edition 2025

Ad maiorem Dei gloriam

www.evelynlinwood.com

My AI Pledge

I do not use generative AI in any stage of my writing process, nor will I ever do so. This applies to Showing Silver and every book that I will ever write or publish.

Art is human.

Showing Silver
BOOK ONE OF THE ARKEN DUOLOGY

EVELYN LINWOOD

Contents

Chapter 1	1
Chapter 2	17
Chapter 3	30
Chapter 4	47
Chapter 5	61
Chapter 6	74
Chapter 7	90
Chapter 8	103
Chapter 9	118
Chapter 10	128
Chapter 11	141
Chapter 12	157
Chapter 13	172
Chapter 14	186
Chapter 15	195
Chapter 16	207
Author Newsletter	215
Acknowledgments	217
About the Author	219

A Map of The Kingdom of Ravena

Dove's Landing
Fort Ravemar
Rothkov
(Greater Duval Holdings)

The Kingdom of Eimar

The Southern Isles
(Shown at Partial Scale)

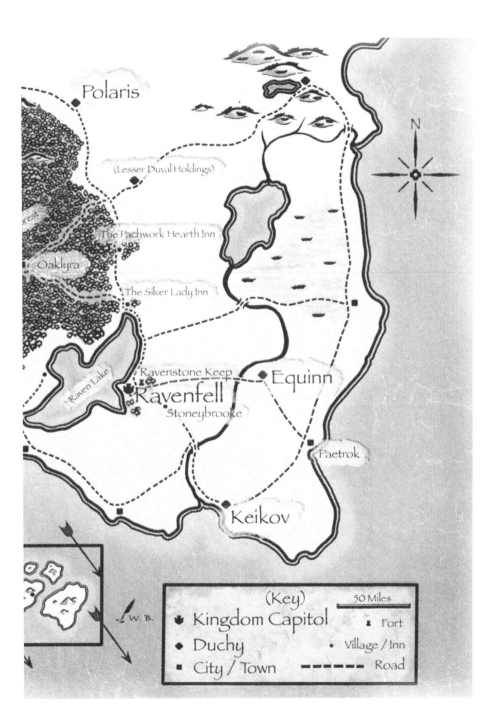

One

Keira pulled her bowstring taut, focusing on the target in her mind's eye. She took a slow, deep breath. There was something calming about the strain of her muscles against the bowstring, even the way the string seemed determined to cut into her fingers. Normally she wore a glove, but it sat forgotten in her room and she hadn't wanted to miss the crispness of the early morning.

Keira could taste the last vestiges of spring as she released the breath, and with it her arrow. It flew true. The thwack of the arrow striking the target brought a smile to her face. It buried itself in the outer edge of the second innermost ring.

Not bad for the first shot of the day. But Keira had not come to practice her archery. Her eyes swept over the empty range with its perfectly manicured grass. Targets made of painted straw were equally spaced at the other side of the range in three groups. Each was further from the archers, with the longest astounding her. Keira hoped she'd get a chance to see the longbowmen practice one of these mornings.

The archery range sprawled at the top of a gradual hill, yet still in the shadow of the castle. Three weeks of living here had not accustomed her to the sight of the stone fortress towering over her. Ravenstone Keep presented an impressive edifice of rough-hewn stone. The crenelated battlement at the top could barely be seen from the ground, but it gave it a militaristic look that Keira was still adjusting to.

A pang of nostalgia for Stoneybrooke, the small town her family had left behind, assailed her, but she shoved it aside. *This is my time to reign it in.* She couldn't waste it, or she'd have a miserable day. Keira could feel her power, thrumming white-hot just below the surface. *It's aggressive today,* she noted.

Keira returned to her meditative breathing. In....out. Slow and deep. She nocked another arrow, trying to clear her mind, and exhaled as she drew the string back. The second shot landed with the same satisfying thwack as the first. She was oddly aware of her body this morning, and the way each draw of the bow stretched and stressed her narrow frame. Her eyes held a special hum, cold and hot at the same time. She knew it meant that her irises were a misty gray at the moment.

They won't turn silver; I won't let them.

Keira continued shooting for nearly an hour. It felt almost like a slow dance. As she focused on the physical, her awareness of her magic dimmed. The tendrils of power that seemed determined to seep out and cause trouble became nothing more than harmless memory. Her eyes returned to their normal frog green.

It seemed to take longer than usual to tame her magic. *Is it because last night's storm kept me from sleeping well?* Keira sighed. There was no use in wondering. She simply didn't know enough about magic to make anything better than a wild guess. She shook her head and nocked another arrow, running through the motion in her mind before raising the weapon.

"I haven't seen you around here before."

Keira whirled, bow safely pointed at the ground.

"I'm sorry. I didn't mean to startle you." A man pushed off of the low stone wall that bordered the target range, uncrossing his arms.

The stranger couldn't be more than a few years older than her nineteen, although his trimmed beard retained none of the patchiness of youth. He was dressed well, in a richly dyed red shirt that she suspected might be a silk blend and light brown pants of velveteen. Still, she doubted that he was a noble. His brown hair was cut in short feathered layers, a style that was popular with the merchant class. She stifled a wave of jealousy at the deep chestnut tone. Her own mouse-brown hair seemed flat in comparison.

Keira gave a polite curtsy, shallow enough for those of equal standing. "We wouldn't have had much chance to meet. My family has lived here only a few weeks."

"In that case, welcome to Ravenstone Keep." He paused and reached out to take her hand. "My name is Fionn Duval."

"Keira Smith." She blushed as he kissed the back of her hand. *Definitely noble. Somebody of my class would just shake my hand.* "A pleasure to meet you milord."

"The pleasure is mine." He gave the barest frown, then his features smoothed over. "Do you shoot often?"

"Daily, if I can help it."

That earned her another smile. "Well, perhaps I'll see you again."

She curtsied again as he left, deeper this time. He nodded in acknowledgment, but she saw his face shift from pleasant to grumpy as he turned away. She was sure she hadn't done anything offensive. *Have I? The last thing I need is to get on the wrong side of a noble.* Lord Fitzroy and his family, who governed Stoneybrooke, had ignored the villagers for the most part, but they had never been unkind. Keira knew, however, that a noble could make all kinds of trouble for her family. Her pa could even lose his position as castle smith, his dream job. *But what can I do? If I did upset him, wouldn't approaching him only make it worse?*

Unable to focus any longer, she unstrung her bow and wrapped it in the scrap of cloth she used to keep it safe. After retrieving her arrows, she trudged down the muddy path to the castle. As she turned into the corridor that led to her family's rooms, Keira froze in horror. *What if he's a duke?* She should have called him 'Your Grace'. But then, if he wasn't she would have looked ridiculous.

The internal debate carried her all the way to her room. After returning her bow and the handful of arrows she owned to the trunk at the foot of her bed, Keira kicked off her boots and collapsed on her narrow bed. She groaned into her pillow, then rolled to her feet. *Tea solves most problems.*

Keira didn't leave her family's rooms again until that afternoon. After sharing a late lunch with her mom, Keira kissed her on the cheek and left her at her sewing. She smiled at the way her mom poked the tip of her tongue out of the corner of her mouth when she was focused, her blonde hair draped forward to cascade over her shoulder.

Keira donned her long brown cloak as she stepped out. She felt a little silly wearing it indoors, but at least it wouldn't clash with the simple green dress she wore. Despite the extravagance of the glass windows that adorned every room of Ravenstone Keep, the stone had not regained the warmth stolen by the long passed winter. At least...she assumed it would grow warmer eventually.

Keira was glad she had missed that season. It would never have occurred to her that their new home might be less comfortable than the old. When her pa had built their former home with his own hands before he married her mom, he had done so with a mind to the comfort of his future bride. The wooden floors had been covered in rugs, each room warm and inviting. It was small, but it was cozy. In contrast, Ravenstone Keep was a sprawling mass of cold, unfeeling stone.

There was one thing that made the move worth it for Keira. Ravenstone Keep's library was famous throughout Ravena, and if rumor was to be believed, all castle residents were permitted to borrow from it. Keira would not believe that without confirmation. Luckily, she had already met one of the librarians. As unmarried women, she and Arielle sat at the same table at dinner. Arielle's parents were entrusted with the keeping of the library, and she helped out as needed. And Keira's new friend had promised to show her around.

Keira found herself bouncing with excitement as she went. She had always enjoyed the few books she had access to. Reading was a pleasant way to pass an afternoon, but books were an uncommon luxury in Stoneybrooke. She couldn't quite remember the directions Arielle had given her, but the library was easy to find. It felt like the castle had a heart and it was drawing her inward.

When she took her first step into the library, Keira stopped in her tracks. She had always believed that people exaggerated when they said a sight stole their breath, but she stood breathless in a vast sea of books. The entire village of Stoneybrooke could be doubled and still fit. Keira forced herself forward, walking steadily toward the center of the cavernous room.

When she reached it, she turned a slow circle. Heavy wooden shelves lined with books stood in wide rows for as far as her eyes could see. Groups of small round tables of sandy wood stood in clearings among the shelves. She stood in the largest of these clearings. Great amber cushions, couches, and chairs lined one wall. The powder blue carpet absorbed most of the sound in the huge chamber. An odd soft hum remained, but it seemed less like a sound than a feeling. The quiet did as much to create a productive atmosphere as the scattered academics reading at the wooden tables.

It was absolutely the most beautiful room Keira had ever seen. The whole place was bathed in a soft, steady light. It was whiter than any she had seen, but soft enough that she didn't feel the need to shield her eyes. Keira imagined that it would delay the eye strain that long stretches of reading by firelight sometimes brought.

But where is it coming from?

Keira's eyes drifted upward as she searched, almost

expecting to find a hole in the ceiling to let in sunlight. She nearly fainted at what she saw instead. The high stone ceiling was obscured by thousands of glowing orbs. They floated along like great pearls of peach, powder blue, and milky white. Each one was roughly the size of a pumpkin. They drifted like clouds until they came too near one of their brethren, then moved apart. It seemed they repelled each other like the wrong end of magnets. Keira wondered if this was the force that had pulled her here. It seemed to be the source of the silent hum that she had sensed.

When her wits returned, Keira walked to the desk in the center of the far wall. It was an odd sort of workspace, forming a wide loop with room for two or three people to work inside it. Arielle was alone behind the desk, ink-stained finger moving down the page of a humongous tome. Her slight frame was dwarfed by the volume. Her long, dark hair was confined to a single thick braid that clung to her scalp and hung over one shoulder. The oil she used to care for it reflected the magical light of the library. Keira hadn't asked her what she used, but it smelled wonderful. Arielle's skin was dusky, despite her long hours spent indoors. She was only seventeen, two years younger than Keira, but she was the best friend she had made here.

Before Keira reached her, the same man she had met at the archery range that morning walked up carrying a stack of books. His clothing settled her previous debate. *He's nobility without a doubt.* Nobody else could afford to be so adorned. He hadn't changed, but had added a decorative cape, clasped over his left shoulder with an ornate piece of gold. The clasp was inlaid with what looked like several small rubies. He also wore several jeweled rings.

The nobleman glanced over as she approached. Keira froze, then bobbed a clumsy curtsy. He smiled, but turned back to Arielle, sliding the heavy pile toward her.

"So few today?" Arielle asked with the ghost of a smile.

"Few?" Keira blurted. She felt her eyes widen and she folded her hands on the desk. It was more books than she had ever seen together before that day.

"Oh, my manners desert me!" Arielle exclaimed, "My lord, may I present Keira Smith?"

Keira managed a much better curtsy.

"Keira, this is Lord Fionn Duval, second son of the Duke of Rothkov." Arielle gestured daintily with one small brown hand.

Keira smoothed her skirt with one hand. Her mouth had gone terribly dry. *How is the son of a duke addressed? Your grace? Your lordship?*

"We were introduced this morning." Lord Duval smirked at Keira, hazel-brown eyes twinkling. "Are you following me?"

"Of course not!" She answered before she had time to realize he was teasing her.

Keira blushed as an awkward silence settled between the trio.

"You must be a great reader, my lord." She commented, just to say something.

Lord Duval shrugged. "I enjoy it as a pastime, but I'm not scholarly."

Keira eyed his stack of books in disbelief, but held her tongue. It seemed he was not fooled.

"I have a friend who never runs out of recommendations." He grimaced. "I feel guilty if I don't at least let them sit on my shelf for a week or two. I do read some of them."

Arielle laughed and her complexion darkened. "Yes, Master Elers has suggested many titles to me."

Arielle pulled the first volumes from the pile, turning them to the inside of the back cover. She removed a small card from a paper pocket attached there and slid them to the side, repeating the process with the next two. When she had set them all to the side, seven cards were arranged on the desk. Keira watched with interest as she stamped each of them. Lord Duval signed in a neat, precise hand. It almost made her blush to think of her own sloppy writing, but then she hadn't had as much practice as a noble would. Paper was so expensive.

"Enjoy your reading, my lord." Arielle said with a smile.

Lord Duval nodded at each of them and left. Arielle slipped the cards into a filing cabinet.

When she turned back and saw the curiosity on Keira's face she explained, "Each book has a unique number that's written on the cards. It's how we track what's been checked out, as well as where to place them on the shelves. Otherwise, we'd never find anything in here."

"Checked out?" Keira asked. She set her hands back on the counter and her eyes flitted from the cabinet to the shelves. *Could I borrow a book on magic without anyone noticing? Surely that would be harmless.*

"Borrowed." She clarified. "His Majesty grants castle residents and the nobility the use of his collection, but you can't simply take something and leave. That's theft. We have to record check-outs so we know if they come back."

"Of course." Keira nodded as if that had been obvious, doing her best to hide the spark of frustration she felt.

It wasn't as if magic was illegal, but she still felt like she was contemplating a crime. Her pa had long ago forbidden her from using her power. It wasn't even as if she didn't agree with him, but it was getting harder to contain. She just wanted to learn enough to pack it away in some forgotten corner of her mind so she could live her life.

Almost as if it objected to her thoughts, her power seemed to bubble up and float just below the surface. Her skin felt too small, and she thought the humming above her grew louder, but when she looked up, the floating lights remained unchanged. She could have collapsed in relief. *Will I need a second archery session today?* She had never needed to center herself twice in one day before.

She wished Brigid had come to the castle too. They had grown up together in Stoneybrooke and she was the only person outside of Kcira's family who knew about her 'gift'. Brigid would leap at the chance to help her borrow magic books. She had always insisted Keira should seek training and be acknowledged as an ArKen.

"They're beautiful, aren't they?" Arielle sighed dreamily. "There are a handful of ArKen living in Ravenstone Keep and they each donate a few globe lights each morning."

A handful? Relieved that Arielle hadn't noticed her panic, Keira agreed. She hadn't known there were ArKen at the castle, but she supposed it made sense. The King probably used them as guards. *But are there any other Naturals?*

"Master Elers can do different colors and he takes requests." Arielle added as she fiddled with the silver locket she wore on a long chain. "Right, books! Where were we?"

"Borrowing them."

Arielle nodded. "Nobility can check out as many books as they choose, but most castle residents are limited to three at a time. I hope you won't be disappointed?"

Keira shook her head, baffled at the idea that she could borrow any, let alone more than one. What if she damaged them?

"What's that look for?"

"I was just wondering how I would ever replace them if something happened."

"I wouldn't worry too much. King Herbert is trying to educate his citizens." Arielle explained, "It's not like there's debtors' prison for lost library books. You simply pay as you can."

"What if 'as you can' is never? Books are so expensive." Keira asked, grimacing.

"You would be limited to reading here if you owed fines, but there's no other penalty." Arielle assured her. "They like to see small payments, but generally the goal is to let more people read more books."

Arielle's library orientation took less time than Keira would have believed. The books were organized simply, with one category slowly blending into another. There were only three real rules. The first two were logical. Of course there was no food because it could damage the books or attract vermin. And Keira already appreciated the quiet and studious atmosphere, so she had no desire to violate it. The last puzzled her exceedingly.

"Why no outside books?"

"They can carry pests. Some insects like to eat paper or glue."

"Oh."

"It's the most important of the rules. We are set up to handle a fire, and food can only damage the books you handle. But if you infect the library, it could cost us the whole collection."

"I have a few books in my rooms. Should I be worried?"

"Freshly returned books are quarantined until they have been cleared."

Arielle turned her loose on the shelves, and Keira did her best to shake the horrific thought of book pests as she browsed. She soon forgot her worries. Within five minutes she had made an important discovery — three books was definitely too few. She gave herself a little mental shake. These books would be here the next time she visited. For now, she needed to find information.

She now knew there would be a record of the books she borrowed. It was silly of her to assume that there wouldn't be, but now she had another obstacle. She needed information on magic, and on ArKen themselves. Keira walked up and down a shelf that seemed to contain relevant tomes, but their titles were all very telling. Many were instruction manuals. Keira sighed and moved to the next shelf, fingers tracing the leather and linen covers. Suddenly she stopped. Her finger rested on A Recent History of ArKen Achievements. Keira felt a smile slowly spread across her face. *History books are harmless, surely?*

Grinning from ear to ear, Keira read the other titles. To her surprise and delight, she found one simply titled 'Naturals'. Flipping through the tome, she found it promising. There was a whole chapter on how Natural ArKen magic manifested. Returning to the first volume, she slipped it on top and headed for the desk. In a moment of panic, she ducked into another section and grabbed the first book her hand touched.

They couldn't all be magic or it would look suspicious. *No. I can't check these out at all.* Keira made her way to an isolated table and started reading. When she was interrupted, she looked up in confusion. It seemed little time had passed, but she had read several chapters. She knew she was reading slower than usual. Many of the lights floating against the ceiling had dimmed or vanished. How much time could have passed?

Arielle stood with one long hand curled around her locket, the other on her hip. "Interesting reading?"

"Wha-? Yes."

Arielle slid into the seat beside her. "It's nearly time for dinner. You *can* take these back to your rooms, you know?"

"I know, but I'm just looking."

Arielle glanced down at the titles and Keira winced before she could stop herself.

Arielle frowned. "Interesting choice of topic."

"Well, you mentioned that there are ArKen in the castle, so I thought I might as well learn about them. In the village..." Keira trailed off, her conscience prickling uncomfortably at the deception.

Arielle stared. It was obvious she had seen through Keira's thin lie. Keira bit her bottom lip. *I've always been so bad at secrets.* She was sure that everyone back in Stoneybrooke at least suspected her burden.

"Curiosity is not to be discouraged," Arielle said, in the manner of someone repeating a proverb. "I hope you aren't afraid of them? I know some people are nervous around those who can wield magic."

"No." Keira gave a half shrug. "But I *am* afraid that I don't remember where I got these."

"That's what those carts are for." Arielle gestured to a wooden shelf on wheels at the end of an aisle, then a haunted look came into her eyes. "The best favor you can do for me and the other library workers is to never re-shelve something if you aren't sure *exactly* where it came from."

Keira nodded solemnly. "I won't." *Which means I'll have to memorize this system if I don't want to get caught satisfying my curiosity about magic.*

* * *

That evening, Keira sat beside Arielle at one of the long wooden tables in the smaller of Ravenstone's two dining halls. They sat with other unmarried women. Most of them had papas employed in and around the castle, like her. Many had found work themselves, leaving Keira feeling a little out of place. *Should I do the same?*

Before the move, she had been training as an herbalist and midwife, but the apprenticeship was left unfinished. She wanted to be of use, but even if she had finished her apprenticeship, Keira's confidence in the herb lore she had been studying was continually decreasing. It had seemed an impossible task to parse the old wives' tales from the true, evidence-based medicine. And now, her hope of a lifetime spent healing people was all but abandoned.

Although Keira knew that the dining hall was considered small by many of the other castle residents, it was enormous in her eyes. She had never seen the great banquet hall, but this room seemed to stretch for a mile. Long wooden tables, like the one where she ate, stretched in three rows through the center of the room. A portion of the floor at the far end was slightly raised, only an inch or two, and a handful of smaller tables were arranged in a wide horseshoe.

Thick banners were draped over the gray stone of the walls. They displayed the coats of arms of nobles who lived in the castle, as well as a few who had performed services for the kingdom, or were in the King's good graces. Keira saw two of them with the thin silver border that marked a house that had produced ArKen. *Naturals?*

She didn't think there was an official distinction between those born with power, Naturals like herself, and the Seekers who studied hard to obtain it. She suppressed a shudder. Why anyone would seek such a burden was beyond her. As her magic fluttered against her skin like a caged bird, she wondered if they ever regretted unlocking their own.

"Dymphna, you're back!" Arielle exclaimed with the widest smile Keira had seen her wear, standing to lean across the table and hug the newcomer around her neck.

After they parted, the blond girl collapsed onto the bench across from them. A light dusting of freckles was scattered across her nose and her wide eyes were the deep blue of the night sky. They looked a little strange because her pale eyelashes were nearly invisible.

Dymphna pushed her bangs away from her forehead. "We only arrived this morning. Who's this?"

"Dymphna, meet Keira. Keira, this is my friend Dymphna." Arielle gestured between them before continuing, "Keira's father is one of the new castle smiths."

"Ah. Welcome." Dymphna smiled, showing dimples and perfectly straight teeth.

"Thank you." Keira glanced down at her stew. "Did you travel far?"

"Not terribly. I'm a ladies' maid and we went to my Lady's country home for a few weeks." Dymphna took a big bite of her dinner, toasted bread smeared with a white cheese and topped with fish.

"Wow. That must have been exciting. Do you get to travel often?" Keira asked.

Dymphna answered with a hand hiding her mouth. "Often enough. Oh! Arielle — you'll never guess what I heard while I was away."

"About Dove's Landing? I heard. I hope your family is well?"

"What? What happened in Dove's Landing?" Dymphna leaned forward as her eyebrows drew down over a pinched expression.

"What's Dove's Landing?" Keira asked in a small voice, feeling rather stupid.

Dymphna's sweet voice sounded oddly strained as she replied, "The village I'm from. It's on the western border. Out with it, Ari."

"It was attacked by bandits."

"What!?"

"I don't think there were many casualties." Arielle assured her, reaching across the table to squeeze her hand. "They had an ArKen with them, and he blew up the wall at the start of it. The villagers cooperated after that. I'm surprised you hadn't heard."

"I'll send a letter today." Dymphna looked down at her breakfast, a shade or two paler for the news.

Keira wanted to ask about her news, but it didn't seem appropriate. She chewed her lip instead.

"What is it?" Dymphna asked. "Speak your mind."

Keira shook her head.

"What was your news?" Arielle asked after an awkward pause.

"Oh. It seems small now. The countryside was wild with rumors about one of the queen's cousins. They say Lady Le Brouche eloped. She hasn't been seen in more than a week."

"Isn't she the one that was supposed to marry the King?" Keira asked, then blushed. "Well, not *supposed to* exactly, but...we thought she would, back in Stoneybrooke."

"Most of the kingdom did." Dymphna confirmed. "Well, even if it's a little...shocking...I'm glad if she found a happy match."

Arielle looked scandalized, and Keira privately agreed with her. An elopement was shameful. *And from a noble no less.* She felt like blushing at the very idea of running off like that, but she was saved from sharing the feeling by a shift in the conversation.

"I have another piece of — far better — news." Arielle said with a barely suppressed smile.

"What's that?" The others chorused.

"I'm going to be a big sister!"

"Isn't your mom too old?" Dymphna straightened in surprise.

Arielle shrugged, but Keira could see the worry that left her shoulders tense. "She has seen a healer, and he assured us that everything should be well as long as she eats properly and gets plenty of rest."

"Not that ArKen?" Dymphna's voice took on a distrustful tone.

Arielle stuck her tongue out. "Yes, *that ArKen*. And we're lucky he was available."

Dymphna shuddered.

"Is he cruel-tempered?" Keira asked, setting her spoon down. Her fingers traced the long grain of the table.

"No." Arielle replied in a clipped tone, but she sighed a moment later.

As Arielle's shoulders relaxed, Keira decided that it was most likely an old argument between the two of them. The disagreement seemed to lack any real heat. She turned a questioning look on Dymphna.

"Magic makes me a little nervous." The other girl admitted, "Don't look at me like that Arielle. It isn't a crime."

"It's natural." Keira agreed, swallowing against a knot that had formed in her throat. It wasn't a lie, exactly. But all the same, she felt herself flush. "Magic is dangerous."

"Magic is wonderful!" Arielle murmured, her dark eyes going wide.

"Wonderful?" Keira snorted.

"ArKen can do amazing things." Arielle insisted, "One or two bad actors doesn't change that."

Dymphna shrugged. "I won't argue with you. And if it helps your mom through her pregnancy, I'll be pleased."

Their meal finished, and the girls said an awkward goodnight and departed for their chambers, but it would be a long time before Keira fell asleep. She laid awake, alternating between marveling at Arielle's attitude toward magic and worrying what Dymphna would think of her, if she knew her secret. *Would it even matter to her that I've chosen not to use my magic?*

Two

The next Free Day, Keira joined her parents for an afternoon ride into the countryside. They still had the sweet, old mule they used for chores around their old home, but he wasn't accustomed to being ridden. Instead, they stopped at a busy stable near the main castle gate and paid a fee to borrow a trio of mounts. It was the first truly hot day of the season and they were sweating by the time they reached their destination. As they approached, an errant piece of cotton-tree fluff drifted into Keira's face. She blew it away, squinting as she watched it float toward a bee-covered patch of flowers. Then she turned and followed her parents inside.

Stepping into the darkness of the stable was a relief from the glare, but it was like stepping into a wall of oppressive humidity. Keira took a slow breath, struggling against the stagnant air. The scents of dirty straw and horse sweat warred for dominance. The human crowd seemed to be conspiring with the horses to make it as hot as possible. She noticed that the horses didn't seem fond of the weather either, but felt some relief when she saw a pair of grooms moving through the barn. One was checking that all of the water buckets were full, while the other stopped to sponge a horse with what she assumed was cool water.

She let her pa choose their mounts. While she thought she knew just as much about horses, the number of finely-dressed people milling around the barn stole her voice. Many of them were dressed like them, in simple though well-made clothes with modest jewelry if they had any. Keira fingered the pink-sand rose that hung on a leather thong around her neck. It was carved from the glass left behind by a lightning strike and came all the way from Rothkov on the coast, whose pink sand beaches were legendary. It would have been unaffordable without the lighter line through the outer petals that showed where it had cracked internally during its journey.

In contrast, some of the members of the crowd seemed to be nobility. Keira found she didn't know how to behave, other than to curtsy if any richly-dressed person met her eyes. Some of them dripped with jewels. *I always thought nobles kept their own horses, but perhaps that's a myth.*

Keira's musings were cut short when her mom shooed her back outside. The temperature immediately dropped several degrees.

"Ladies' choice." Her pa said, holding up a trio of reins.

Her mom claimed the reins of a small, gray mule. Keira glanced between the two remaining mounts — a dark brown mule that was chewing on his lead and a tall, dapple gray horse. She smiled and took the mule. His attention immediately shifted to her as he hunted for treats in hidden pockets.

She rewarded his efforts with a small apple and a scratch behind his nearest ear. "You're a friendly one, aren't you?"

The mule responded by nearly bowling her over as he leaned into her hand. *A little too friendly.*

Keira and the others mounted and set off. They chose a shady lane along the inside of the castle wall, and Keira breathed a sigh of relief. The heavy scent of a lilac tree made her nose itch. They seemed to have bloomed late this year, but Keira loved the look of them. She suspected the light purple of being one of her favorite colors, second only to a rather specific shade of deep green.

As she admired them, her magic stirred. *No stop; not now!* The mule froze and Keira loosened her legs. She focused on taking deep breaths and the rough texture of the reigns in her hands. *This is fine, I'm fine.* The mule seemed to sense her begin to relax, and it walked after the others. *Thank goodness I was taking up the rear.* Keira didn't want to bother her parents with this, not on her pa's only day off — and when there was nothing he could do.

Her pa led the way downhill toward an open space. Keira smiled at the thought of letting the mule stretch its legs properly, and then remembered the weather. She groaned internally. *It would be best if we stick to a walk.* She returned to her breathing. She closed her eyes, trusting the mule to follow the group as she shoved her magic deeper. The mule gave a little shake of its ears, but seemed to be moving in the right direction.

What is it about archery that helps so much? Keira asked herself, still fighting rising panic. *Familiarity? Repetition? Physical Exertion?* She focused on the feel of her muscles as she balanced on the mule. It snorted at her, and Keira opened her eyes. The worst had passed, but she needed something she could do during the day. Her little problem was getting bigger.

"Keep up!" Her mom called to her.

Keira looked up and found that she had fallen behind. She urged her mount into a brief trot to catch up, and soon joined her parents in the open field. There, they found a stream. Despite their relaxed pace, their mounts were thirsty. Keira slid to the ground to let her little mule cool off. He seemed to be radiating heat. Her parents did the same.

"This is nice." Keira's mom smiled dreamily, leaning against her somewhat sweat-marked husband as he absentmindedly looped an arm around her waist.

Keira fought to hide her reaction. *Parents.*

"I've been at the forge more than I'm used to." Her pa said, a thoughtful look on his face as he turned to her. "We've now been here a full month. How are you settling in?"

Keira smiled. "I've made a couple of friends, and you won't hear me complain about the library."

"Good." Her mom smirked. "I did see you with a stack of books."

"But Pa, are you pleased with your work?" Keira stroked her mule's long ears as she waited for his answer.

"Very. I'm even up for my first real commission."

"Truly Liam?" Her mom spun to face him.

He grinned like a teenager hoping to impress his crush as his voice took on a teasing tone. "I had quite the imperious visitor yesterday. No lower than a duchess."

"Impossible!" Keira and her mom chorused.

He puffed up further. "Possible. She was searching for a smith to craft something for her son's birthday. I'm to produce a few daggers so she can see what I can do."

Keira bit her lip. *Isn't that a lot for one job?*

"And are you the only one?"

Her papa gave an exaggerated pout and drew out her mom's name with a slight whine, "Estelle, don't ruin the effect on the impressionable youth present."

"Oh, right." She winked.

"There are a few smiths doing the same, but even if I'm not chosen, there seems to be a decent market for such things. And we were promised compensation for the materials and time."

There was no other word for it; Keira was astounded. To think that her pa had already attracted the eye of such a customer. *He really is living his dream.* Her eyes grew misty and she had to lean against her mule and resume her breathing exercises to avoid a magical surprise. She smiled. *Ambition like his so rarely pays off.*

"Are you alright?" Her mom set a cool hand on her cheek. "You should speak up when it's important."

"I'm fine. Perhaps a bit overheated."

"Maybe we should head back?" Her mom looked at her pa.

He gave a huff of agreement and mounted his large horse.

* * *

Late that night, Keira lounged against the door to their old cart mule's stall, absentmindedly stroking Cinnamon's velvet ears. When they returned from their afternoon ride, she had found sanctuary from the heat deep within the castle walls. She found an unoccupied table in the library and read for hours. Anatomical sketches still swam in her mind. Despite shadowing their midwife for months before leaving Stoneybrooke, she had never known the human body had so many parts.

A door closed somewhere to Keira's right, startling her. Cinnamon blew in her ear, lipping at her collar. Keira gave him one last pat before investigating the source of the noise. At the end of the aisle, she discovered a stable boy sitting on the ground, talking to an older stable hand and a man she didn't recognize.

The stranger's looks were a stark contrast to the weathered and muscular stablehand. He was tall, thin, fair, and dressed in expensive fabrics. He seemed horribly out of place in the stable. The stranger sank to his knees, and Keira thought she could read concern in the slight wrinkle between his brows, although it could also have been irritation.

Keira paused, embarrassed. The boy shifted on the ground, tears of pain glistening on his cheek as the tall, well-dressed man reached for his quickly purpling leg. The boy's pant leg had already been cut away to reveal a bloody hoof print on a swollen thigh. Keira flushed, but did not look away as the stranger examined the wound.

He paused for a moment with his eyes closed before reporting, "His femur is fractured. It's a small break, but such a large bone will take time to heal."

"Even after you're done, Master Elers?" The older stable hand asked in surprise.

The interaction confirmed Keira's suspicions. The tall man was an ArKen. Almost without thinking, Keira took a step closer.

The stranger gave a curt nod.

"Please do what you can."

"Healing can hurt." The stranger warned the boy, bending over his leg.

Keira ignored the silent hum that filled the air and watched in fascination as the leg returned to normal size. The stable boy cried out, then he seemed to droop with exhaustion. The worst of the bruising faded and the skin knit slowly together. Finally, the ArKen leaned back, removing large hands to examine his work.

The healer turned to the older stable hand. "It is essential that he do no work for the next seven days. Not light work, *no* work." He drew himself up to his full height and stared the man down.

The older man visibly swallowed and then gave a shallow bow. "Yes m'lord."

"And he'll need to take it easy when he does return."

Turning back to the boy, he instructed, "Try to stay off the leg for the next few days. The bone is whole, but it will take a while for it to fully heal. You could easily re-injure yourself. Can you imagine, all that pain for nothing?" He teased.

The boy scrubbed at the tear tracks on his sweaty face. "Thank you Master Elers. I'll be careful."

Elers inclined his head and told him to get some rest, stretching as he watched the stable workers go, the young supported by the older. The whole thing had taken nearly an hour, Keira realized as she watched the fading light of the retreating pair's lantern. Master Elers leaned against a nearby stall for a moment before turning and nearly flattening her.

He caught Keira just in time and bowed. "Excuse me, miss."

She curtsied low in response, still in awe over what she had just witnessed.

"Are you alright?" He asked, misreading her expression. "Can I get you some water?"

"Oh no. I'm fine. Thank you for your kind concern m-m'lord." Her voice came out oddly breathy.

With an inclination of his head, he offered her his arm, "May I escort you back to the castle?"

"Thank you, my lord." Keira swept him another clumsy curtsy before accepting his arm.

The pair headed for the castle in silence. Keira could not forget what she had seen; if she could only learn one use for her magic, it would be this. She could hardly imagine — to be able to take away another person's hurts, maybe even save their life. Her power thrummed just below the surface, and for once, Keira didn't mind the feeling.

"Is healing very difficult magic?"

"Pardon me?" Master Elers looked down at her as if he had almost forgotten she was there.

"I know magic in general is hard to work properly, but is healing especially difficult?"

He took a while to answer, and Keira was glad he seemed to be taking her question seriously.

"That would depend on who you ask. I believe most ArKen would say that it is. Personally, I have found it easier than other things." He shrugged. "The body wants to be whole."

"I wish I could do that."

"Anyone can learn; it's just a matter of dedicated application." He paused, considering, "If it's something you want to pursue, let me know. I could be of some use Miss...?"

"Smith. Keira Smith."

"Well, if you do?"

Keira felt herself go pale.

"Then again, maybe you don't. Goodnight Miss Smith." He released her arm and bowed. They had reached one of the many entryways to the castle.

"Goodnight, Master Elers." She returned with a curtsy she knew was too deep. "Thank you."

* * *

Keira lay awake, watching the shadow of her curtains dance on her ceiling. It was a breezy night, and the steady whine of the wind did nothing to quiet her thoughts. She had never seen magic like that before. She rolled over, snuggling deeper into her covers. Of course, she'd known it was *possible* to heal with magic, but knowing and seeing were two very different things. And she had never imagined it could be that effective.

'Magic is dangerous.' — She must have heard those words a million times. Keira had no doubt that it could kill, purposefully or even by accident. For the most part, she had always dismissed magic as a foolishly risky pursuit. From her limited experience, it was generally used to make life easier — for luxury more than anything. Somehow, she had never thought about the things that only magic could do. That stableboy would have lost his position by the time he recovered, if he fully recovered at all.

What if magic was easier to control than she realized? Master Elers had sounded so confident that anyone could learn. If she could be certain that her magic wouldn't hurt anyone....Keira would give almost anything to be able to heal.

And I could help keep people like Arielle's mom, pregnant later in life, safe. Keira bit her lip. Her own magic seemed to thrum just under the surface, swirling in time with her thoughts. She could almost imagine it seeping out to fill her room with tendrils of possibility.

Keira was surprised to find her eyes wet. She rolled over again, stubbornly shoving the feeling down and watching the curtain dance instead of its shadow. It had been hours since she'd seen Master Elers heal the stable boy, but nothing had changed. She didn't have any answers and she knew she needed more information, but sneaking around wouldn't feel right. She'd speak to her parents in the morning, she decided.

With that, she found it easier to sleep. Her magic still swirled, but less aggressively as Keira drifted into an uneasy dream. She slept lightly enough to feel herself toss in bed. Her arm was scratched by the coarse corner of her quilt and a memory seeped into her dreams.

Keira was twelve again, reading from her favorite book of

tales. It was well past her bedtime and the only light came from a flickering candle on her bedside table. It guttered, threatening to go out, and in a troll-headed moment Keira decided to keep it alive. She closed her eyes, feeling her internal flame flicker in time with the fire. All she had to do was draw a little out...*no....not that much!*

Keira was frozen in place as her dream departed from her memory. This time, nobody came. Fire leaped from her to the candle, burning a dark trail across the beautiful green quilt her grandmother and aunts had sewn for her when she was small. Tears sprang to her eyes, but the heat of the flames kept her face dry. She couldn't breathe, couldn't call out for help. The book burned. The bed burned. The world burned around her, leaving her dry and hot. Just as the floor began to collapse beneath her, Keira woke with a start.

She looked around in sweaty terror, expecting to find destruction all around her. Instead, heart still thudding against her breastbone, she looked out over her small, dark bedroom. It seemed like there were tendrils of power stretching away in every direction. She wanted a light to dismiss the silly notion, but at the moment the thought of lighting a candle was too frightful. Instead, she threw the covers off and crawled onto the cool, solid stone of the castle floor. She breathed slowly, trying to calm herself.

After a few minutes, she felt better. *It was just a dream.* Keira rolled over to find another cool patch of floor. *Do I have a fever?* She laid there for a little while, unsure how late it was. She didn't have to wait long for an answer. She noticed the sky lightening at the same moment that she heard her mom in the next room making her pa's morning tea.

At least her nightmare had a silver lining. *I might be an early bird, but I almost never get to see him in the mornings these days.* Keira pulled herself into a sitting position, then rolled to her feet. She bounced on her toes, feeling odd and loose, but pulled on the first linen skirt that touched her hand. It was deer-brown and swishy. She always felt just a little bit fancy in it, as the skirt was wider than typical for her station. To tone that effect down a little, she added her leather vest on top of an undyed shirt. Matching leather boots and her rose necklace completed the ensemble.

Keira paused at the door, suddenly nervous. Would they be able to see it? Her magic was still awake, just beneath the surface. It wasn't the first such day, but they were coming more frequently. She sighed and stepped into the sitting room, knowing that she would have to mention it.

"Good morning." Her own voice sounded too bright in her ears.

Her mom looked at her with sharp eyes. "Is something on your mind?"

"Yes, I..." Keira paused, caught unprepared. She fumbled, looking for the words to explain.

Her parents sat beside each other on their overlarge sofa. Her pa's arm was draped over her mom's shoulders, his other hand caressing her mom's hand. Her mom took a sip of steaming tea with her free hand, leaning back against the dark brown fabric, her head resting in the crook of her husband's arm.

"I'm having trouble finding the words. It's about my magic." Keira fell silent at the look on her pa's face.

"We've already settled that matter."

"Evidently not." Her mom leaned forward. "What is it, darling?"

"I need to..." She trailed off, the worried look on her pa's face distracting her.

"Liam!" Her mom cajoled, tapping his chest with the back of her hand.

He sighed. "Go on Keira, we're listening."

"I need to learn more about magic."

Her pa started to interrupt, but Keira's mom put a hand on his shoulder.

"It isn't that I want to learn to use it, but I need to understand it better. Pa, I saw something amazing last night. A healer in the stables — if you had seen that boy's leg...I-I could learn to do that. Maybe."

Her mom hid a smile. "What happened to 'I don't want to learn to use it'?"

Keira made a funny noise in her throat. "I don't. Well...I don't really know."

Her pa got up to pour her a mug of tea. "Come sit with us. I'm not trying to deny you anything, Sprout. Why do you think I never wanted you to learn?"

"Because 'magic is dangerous.'" She mumbled to her boots before accepting a warm teacup and settling into the padded rocking chair across from them, her booted toes digging into the thick bearskin rug at their feet.

"That's part of it, but it isn't the main reason. You remember your Aunt Rose?"

"Of course." It had been nearly a decade since they'd met, but her pa's sister had been her favorite aunt as a child.

"You know that she's a Natural, like you?"

Keira nodded.

"She's lived a lonely life. When she began her studies, a great many people pulled away from her."

"Keira," her mom added, "being your mother is the most fulfilling thing I've done with my life, and I know you love children. If you become an ArKen, the chances of having your own are...almost nonexistent."

"I don't see why that should be." Keira said as she fought not to scowl.

"Nobody wants an ArKen to marry into their family," her pa explained, "Magic may be useful, but it's dangerous. And having the same rights and status as a noble is not quite the same as actually *being* one."

"I didn't realize," she breathed, "but I think I should have at least some say in the matter. It's my magic we're talking about."

"Of course, honey." Her mom gripped her pa's hand tightly. "But he's right. It would change your life entirely."

"And it's me who'd have to live with that."

"So what are you asking?" Her pa reached out to hold her hand.

She looked down at her small calloused hand in his giant one. "For permission to learn enough to know what I want. I've been reading a bit, but I don't want to do more without your permission."

"Reading?" Her parents asked in unison.

"Yes. Nothing instructive. I just...I don't know *anything*... about what magic can do. About how hard it is to control, and if I'd be better off learning to use mine." She squeezed his hand tighter. "That's not all. I have to fight not to use it, and it's been getting harder."

"What do you mean?" Her mom came to put an arm around her shoulders.

"Well...it's like if I don't pay attention it will...slip out. I can feel the magic just below the surface. Some days, it's like calm water, others I swear if I breathe too hard something will happen."

"If it was still like that, you should have told us." Her pa admonished.

Keira shrugged. "You don't like to talk about my magic."

"Yes, well." He frowned into his teacup, looking away. "I thought it would have gone away."

Keira laughed. "I'm a Natural. The one thing I know for sure is that it will never go away. But if I learn a little more, maybe I'll find something that will help me quiet it down."

After a long silence, punctuated with meaningful looks between her parents, her pa spoke again.

"Very well. If you need to understand it better, that's reasonable. I'll look into things and..." He started patting his pockets like he was looking for something.

"Thank you Pa, but my friend Arielle will help me in the library."

"You told her!?" Her mom gasped.

"No, but I think I must. She knows the library better than anyone, and she's not afraid of ArKen."

"Would you really trust her with your secret?" Her mom asked, leaning toward her with a serious expression on her face.

"Yes. It isn't as if I've done anything wrong, even if it does get out."

"That's true, but it would be a bigger-" Her mom started.

"I think it's a good idea." Her pa said at the same time.

"Really?" Keira and her mom chorused.

He nodded firmly. "She has to have someone. Don't you think, my dear?"

A long minute of silence followed before her mom reluctantly agreed.

Keira kissed them each on the cheek and dashed to the door before he could change his mind, and tossed a quick, "Thank you!" over her shoulder before pulling the door shut behind her.

She stood in the hall, shocked at her success. Then, after collecting her wits, Keira jogged in the direction of the library. As always, she seemed drawn there as if by a magnet, but today she was certain it was her own excitement.

Three

When Keira arrived in the library, she found it empty and much darker than on her previous visits. She had never come so early. The doors were open, but the lights had not been renewed. A mere handful of the incandescent orbs floated stubbornly, smaller and paler than Keira had yet seen them. She inched forward, squinting through the empty darkness and half expecting to be told the library was closed.

Keira gained a little confidence when nobody stepped from behind a shelf to admonish her. She reached the middle of the cavernous room before she encountered anyone else. There, a pair of scholars shared a flameless lantern. It looked much like one of the floating orbs trapped in a glass box with a handle.

She stared until one of them looked up, frowning at the interruption. She curtsied and fled between the aisles. Keira didn't stop to think where she was going and was soon lost. She came to a stop in an unfamiliar section of the library.

The nearest shelf was packed with nearly identical volumes. They were all bound in black leather, and the silver titles stamped on their sides reflected the scant light. Keira reached up and grabbed the nearest one, surprised that it wasn't heavier. She turned it over so she could squint at the front cover. In curling silver font, it read:

Observations on Weather Phenomena
by Mistress Selene Morgan.

An ArKen wrote this!! Keira clutched the precious volume against her chest, greedy eyes scanning the other titles. They included such things as *The Life Cycle of the Common Minnow*, *Mathematic Formulae of Energy Conversion*, and *The Grain Shortage of 1215, How it Could Have Been Prevented and Remedied*. Keira pulled a few volumes down and found that they were all written by a Master or Mistress.

She had stumbled upon a collection of ArKen-written works. She didn't recognize the names of any of the authors, but it seemed a real treasure trove. She spent the next ten or fifteen minutes looking for something relevant, or at least interesting, but she had no luck. The entire collection seemed to be painfully detailed work with so many unknown words that she would have to spend a full day deciphering a single page.

The one exception was the first book that she had picked up. It was at least readable, so Keira carried it to a table near the scholars. She was hoping that their light would help her see the pages, but it was still difficult unless she angled her book perfectly to catch the glow. She bent to read the table of contents, then flipped to chapter one. *I'll just read until Arielle gets here.*

Four thick chapters later, Keira looked up to find the library fully lit. *Drat.* She had hoped to see the floating lights made. *How much time has passed?* It was impossible to tell, but she realized with a start that she had read nearly two hundred pages. The book was written with such whimsy and humor that Keira felt the same way she did when reading her favorite fairy stories. What's more, she was sure she remembered most of the information.

Keira shut the book with a heavy sigh. Her shoulders popped as she stretched. *What a relief!* She hadn't realized that she had been so hunched. She tucked the thick book into the crook of her elbow and went in search of Arielle.

It wasn't a lengthy search. Arielle sat on a tall stool behind the counter, fiddling with her locket. Her eyes were unfocused and filled with worry. Keira greeted her, speaking softly so she wouldn't startle, and Arielle reciprocated.

"Are you worrying about your mom again?"

"Yes." She dropped her locket and gave a subtle shake of her head. "Not a very productive use of my time."

Keira couldn't help but smile a little. "It's understandable."

"I wish she would just agree to see the healer again. She's insisting that the midwife is enough. I don't understand it."

"I do. I'm not sure I'd want to see an ArKen, if I could help it. And she's not that old. Lots of people have babies a little late."

"She's forty-six!"

"Truly?"

Arielle nodded, black eyes glittering. "I have four older siblings, all grown."

"Well...give her time to come around." Keira's said, regretting the empty phrase as soon as she spoke it.

"There's little else I can do." Arielle sighed and stood, orange skirt swishing. "Did you want to check that out?"

"What?" Keira looked down. "Yes. But...can we talk privately?"

"I can get away with an early lunch break if you'd like to join me?"

Keira nodded, biting her lip. Arielle's practiced hands went through the motions of checking out the book, then stopped suddenly.

"You have good taste! I've never been particularly interested in the weather, but I could listen to Mistress Morgan talk about it for hours."

She handed the book to Keira. The silver lettering gleamed rosy and Keira glanced up. The colors had changed. Today, it was a mix of red and a soft blue-white, interspersed with an occasional over-large orb in a violent shade of purple. It gave her another twinge of regret for missing their creation. Whoever made the purple orbs might be a rather fun person. *Wait...did Arielle just say she knows the author?*

"What's on your mind?" Arielle asked, looping her arm through Keira's free elbow.

Keira didn't answer, so Arielle led her through a wooden door into a small room designed for work breaks. It was home to a pair of comfortable armchairs by a glowing fireplace, a small larder, and a tiny round table with three stools, each upholstered in a bright orange that matched the fiery rug stretched across the stone at their feet. Arielle's bold skirts fit right in.

Keira sat in one of the armchairs while Arielle prepared a cold lunch and hot tea. She rubbed her thighs nervously and started to stand, feeling like she should be helping. Arielle waved her back into her seat, joining her in only a few minutes.

"I'm a Natural." Keira blurted as soon as the hot teacup touched her fingertips.

Perhaps not the best timing, she realized as Arielle's hand twitched in surprise. The other girl only narrowly avoided spilling scalding tea all over her outstretched hands.

"An ArKen?" Arielle breathed, taking a small step backwards.

"No!" Keira hissed, more harshly than she intended. She sighed, resting a hand over her eyes. "I'm untrained."

"Why?" Arielle slid into the remaining armchair.

Keira shrugged. "Magic is dangerous."

When Arielle looked unconvinced, Keira relayed her last disastrous attempt at magic. She may not have burned the house down like she did in her nightmares, but she did catch her quilt on fire — something she counted as a precious family heirloom. Luckily, her pa heard her scream and was quick to smother the flames.

"But that sounds like a success!" Arielle pointed out as she handed her a cup of tea. "You asked for fire, and you got it."

"I wasn't trying to burn my bed!" Keira exclaimed, "Besides, my pa has forbidden me to learn...even if I wanted to."

"Do you?"

Keira spun the teacup in her hands. "I don't know. I don't think so. It was never an option."

"Then why have you been reading about ArKen?"

"You noticed that?"

Arielle chuckled. "Don't worry. I'd be the only one."

"I'm trying to find out how to get rid of it."

"Your magic!? You can't! Don't *ever* try!" The depth of panic in Arielle's dark eyes brought Keira up short.

"I-I don't really mean get rid of it, just...learn to ignore it? It feels like...a pebble in your shoe, but in my mind. It's hard to keep in line sometimes."

Arielle leaned back in her chair, offering Keira a cold sandwich before taking one for herself. She tilted her head. "Maybe you can ask one of the castle ArKen for help. You don't have to become an apprentice to ask a question."

"Do you know Mistress Morgan?" Keira tapped the book in her lap.

"I've known her most of my life. She wouldn't be my first choice of helper though, not for a Natural."

"Why's that?"

Arielle squirmed a little in her seat. "I mean this in the nicest way possible, but she's a bit...eccentric?"

Keira nodded. A predictable ArKen was intimidating enough.

Arielle must have read something in her face, "No, I'm saying this badly. She's a sweetheart, but Mistress Morgan has her particular interests. And she knows everything about those, but she isn't a Natural and as far as I know she's never taken a special interest in them. I'm sure she would welcome the company if you want to ask her some questions. I just don't know how useful she'd be."

"What about Master Elers? Have you ever spoken with him?"

"He borrows a lot of books." Arielle said, her brown face turning distinctly red. Her entire face seemed to grow a shade or two darker and rosier, rather than her cheeks.

Keira couldn't recall seeing her blush before. A sly smile slid into place. "So...what do you think of him?"

"He's brilliant." Arielle sighed, her blush fading. "And really nice, even if he is a bit clueless."

"Clueless?" Keira asked.

The blood rushed back into her friend's face. "He hasn't noticed um..."

Her friend's voice got too quiet for Keira to hear, but she was fairly certain she had just admitted to flirting. She couldn't help but giggle, and Arielle joined in.

"I saw him heal someone. Maybe you should ask him to check in on your mom?"

"He was the one who saw her before, but I can't...not when she doesn't want me to."

Keira squeezed her hand in understanding. "You won't tell anyone my secret, right?"

"I'd sooner lie to a griffin." Arielle said solemnly. "I do have to get back to work though."

"You barely touched your lunch!"

"Oh." Arielle looked down at the sandwich in her hand, missing only one small bite. She took another. "Master Elers really is handsome."

"Is he a noble?" Keira probed.

Arielle shrugged, taking a rather larger bite of her lunch.

"I suppose the rules change a bit with ArKen."

Arielle swallowed. "They do. And he isn't a first son or anything. A third, from a minor house. My family is...respectable, although untitled."

Keira thought her heart would break, seeing the way Arielle's thin shoulders drooped. "And things are different with ArKen."

"They are!" Arielle brightened a little. "He wouldn't even need his family's approval to marry beneath him, although I imagine he'd want it."

Keira's eyes widened. She really had chosen the right person to confide in. If her friend was willing to *marry* an ArKen, then she'd have no troubles remaining friends with one.

"Oh! I just...it isn't. He hasn't." Arielle stammered, misunderstanding her surprise.

"It's alright. Secrets were made to be traded between friends." Keira squeezed her hand.

Arielle grinned, then popped the rest of her sandwich in her mouth as she stood. She took another quick sip of tea before looking around.

"I'll clean up. You can get back to work."

"Thanks."

Keira gave a little wave and leaned back in her chair. She sighed. *That went better than I expected.*

She sipped her tepid tea for a few minutes before pulling herself to her feet to clean up. *Why am I so tired today?* But she knew the answer. Maintaining a grip on her magic, especially when she was feeling strong emotion, was wearing her down. And it was getting worse. *I don't know how I can do this for the rest of my life.*

* * *

During the following month, Keira invested a great deal of time in reading. Some of it was spent hunched over tables in the library. The light was better there, perfect really, but she couldn't shake the feeling that she was doing something almost criminal.

Most of her time was spent holed up in her family's rooms, sipping tea with her mom and sitting in odd positions while she studied. With anyone else, she would have sat properly, but her mom just smiled and kept sewing, even when Keira laid with her back on the floor and her feet on the couch, her wide skirt failing to conceal her lower legs.

Arielle helped when she could, but she was busy doing as much of the heavy lifting in the library as she could manage. Keira could tell she was worried. While Arielle never mentioned it, she was certain she was trying to keep her mom away from physical labor. Keira tried to help, but she wasn't good for much more than company at first. The shelving system was simple on its surface, but the catalog was huge. She simply didn't know her way around well enough to be useful. Arielle thanked her anyway and the pair of them indulged in whispered conversations while Arielle shelved books from their cart, stifling disruptive laughter as necessary.

Sometimes, for a bit of variety, Keira would join Arielle in Dymphna's room. The others sewed and Keira tried to read until she realized she was doing more talking than page turning. Inevitably, she would join them in their sewing. Dymphna was a ladies' maid, so there was always sewing to be done.

Most of what Keira read was difficult to understand. She found books filled with ancient or foreign runes, complicated diagrams, and wordings so esoteric as to be nearly unintelligible. Arielle was able to translate one set of ancient runes, but Keira's progress was slow.

What she did understand was unhelpful. Keira didn't want to know how to use magic. She wanted to know how to shut it up. Her own power had never been so troublesome. Keira hoped it was just because that's where her focus was, but her magic pulsed just below the surface of her mind, ready to jump at the slightest provocation. Her morning archery sessions had never been more necessary, or less effective. Some days required an evening session as well...most days, if she was honest with herself.

Keira shuddered as she turned the page, remembering the fire. After a few more minutes of struggle, she straightened and looked around. As always, her eyes were drawn to the library ceiling, with its unusual ornamentation. The orbs were different colors now — gold, green, and a subtle brown. She wondered idly if they changed with the season — they had reached the height of summer — or if it was according to the mood of whomever made them.

"Copper for your thoughts?" A man sank into the chair

across from her, splitting his stack of books in half so they could see each other.

"I was just admiring the ceiling lights."

"Oh, I thought it might be something you read."

"What? Oh — " Keira looked across the table to find Lord Fionn Duval sitting there. Most of his rings were missing, but there was no mistaking the midnight blue velveteen he wore as anything less than a noble's attire. She gulped. "No m'lord."

Keira snapped her book shut and immediately regretted it. She was reading one of the special books, bound in black leather, with it's title stamped in clear silver letters across the front. Naturally, the title was as revealing as possible: *An Introduction to the Arcane*. Lord Duval almost seemed amused by her reading choice, but he didn't comment.

Keira set a hand over the title. "I'm just a little curious."

"Far be it from me to dampen anyone's curiosity. If you'd like, I can introduce you to a real ArKen — a magic user, that is."

"I know what an ArKen is," she said, bristling. "I'm not a bumpkin, just because I'm from a country village."

He sat back in his seat and frowned.

Keira could have kicked herself. Why was she being so defensive? *I can't afford to give affront to a noble.* She didn't have much personal experience with nobility. Lord Fitzroy, the governor of Stoneybrooke, would never have sat down so casually with a peasant. But she had heard stories. Everyone knew that a noble could ruin your life as easy as blinking.

Lord Duval rested his head in his hand, elbow on the table. "My friend enjoys answering questions almost as much as he likes asking them."

"Your friend, my lord?" Keira's pulse quickened.

"Yes. I'm close with one of the castle ArKen. Master Elers." He rolled his eyes. "Which sounds stuffy as a carriage at noon in summer. He's just Declan."

Keira gripped the edges of her book tightly, glancing down at the dark cover. "Oh...no I don't think I could. I..."

He waited for her to continue, no sign of irritation crossing his face.

Keira swallowed hard. "He's...frightening."

Lord Duval scowled. "Declan has never done anything to earn that word."

"Oh! No...I didn't mean..." Keira mumbled. "He's so tall..."

The nobleman laughed. "Tall?"

"Talented." Keira said, shrinking against her chair. "I saw him heal someone a few weeks ago."

Lord Duval gave a teasing smile. "And that makes him intimidating?"

"Yes. I could never ask someone like him about what amounts to a passing curiosity." She pushed the book aside for emphasis, waiting for him to leave.

But he lifted a book from one of his piles. "I hope you don't mind the company."

"No, of course not milord." Keira managed.

Lord Duval read quietly. After a moment, Keira returned to her reading as well, but his presence was distracting. He stayed for nearly two hours, during which she managed to read only a few pages. He kept glancing up at the wrong moments and catching her watching him. She couldn't imagine Lord Fitzroy joining her for an afternoon of reading. And Lord Fionn Duval was quite a bit more handsome than Lord Fitzroy. She had no idea how to behave.

Keira flipped to a new section, embarrassed by how little she had read. To her surprise, she found a set of simple, easy-to-follow instructions for creating a globe light like the ones that floated above their heads. She looked up again, craning her neck to see as many of them as possible.

"Is the ceiling really that interesting?" Lord Duval asked with a smile in his voice.

She returned her attention to their table, ignoring the slight dizziness from looking up, and slid her book toward him. "I didn't expect to find such a thing just lying around in a book."

His lips twitched. "Where else would you find it?"

Keira shrugged. "In an apprenticeship."

"Some ArKen study on their own for years before finding a Master," he explained, "It might be discouraged, but it isn't illegal."

"Oh." Keira frowned. "That doesn't sound safe."

"From what Declan tells me, it isn't."

"Even for Naturals?" Keira asked before she could stop to think.

"Especially for Naturals!" Lord Duval exclaimed, then narrowed his eyes.

Keira shrugged. "I wouldn't know."

Arielle came bouncing into view, slightly out of breath. "I've come to liberate y-oh! Hello Lord Duval." She curtsied.

"Good afternoon, Miss Black. I should be going anyway. I've taken too much of your friend's time." He quirked a smile at Keira that made her heart race before standing and bowing to the pair of them.

Keira remembered her manners at the last moment and rose to curtsy as he walked by.

"What was that?" Arielle asked.

Keira shrugged, "He joined me for some reading. The other tables were full, I suppose."

"They weren't." Arielle waggled her eyebrows.

"Staahp." She gave the other girl's shoulder a little shove. "You know perfectly well he wouldn't be an option for me."

"He would if you trained your magic."

Keira blushed. "I doubt it. And what was that about liberating?"

"Would you like to meet an ArKen?"

"Right now?" Her heart sped for a new reason.

Arielle grinned and spun on her heal, walking backwards as she raised her eyebrows. Keira scooped up her books and hurried to follow.

* * *

"You're sure she won't mind the interruption?" Keira asked, smoothing her plain skirt with a suddenly sweaty hand. "I'm just a blacksmith's daughter."

"Selene won't mind." Arielle led Keira deeper into the rows of shelves.

Mistress Morgan's office was tucked away in an alcove far from the busier sections of the library. Two twisting stone columns flanked the heavy wooden door. It was isolated enough for Keira to question Arielle's certainty about interruptions, but she kept her peace.

Instead, she knocked softly on the door. No answer came and the girls stood there for a few moments.

Arielle pressed her ear to the door, then knocked again. "Mistress Morgan!" She called softly.

A moment later the door cracked open, "Arielle! Come in - sit! I'll make us some tea. Just give me a moment."

She left the door wide and returned to her office, still talking, "You have excellent timing. I'm working on another set of copies and my hand was starting to cramp."

Mistress Morgan stretched and yawned languidly, one hand tangled in her long, black hair. She moved a pile of papers off of one chair and poured two mugs of tepid water. Keira looked around at the chaos that was her office. Stacks of paper were everywhere, and there was a crooked pile of books on the floor in one corner. The desk wasn't so much a pile as a disaster area. Keira was amazed Mistress Morgan managed to get any work at all done in a place like this.

"We'll need three mugs." Arielle said, smiling.

"Three?" Mistress Morgan blinked.

"This is my friend Keira." Arielle pushed her forward.

"A pleasure to meet you, Mistress Morgan." Keira curtsied.

"Selene, please."

Arielle poured a third cup of water as Selene ushered Keira to a seat. Keira had to move a small pile of books to the floor. The Mistress didn't see. She had turned to the tea cups. Keira watched in awe as her dark eyes faded to a dull silver for a moment and steam began to rise from the cups. Mistress Morgan served her guests before resuming her own seat. Keira accepted her tea gratefully, wrapping her fingers around its warmth in amazement.

"You have auspicious timing, my dears," Mistress Morgan said through another yawn, "I was in great need of a break."

"Selene, you *do* know you can take one any time?" Arielle teased, "It isn't as if you have a deadline."

She laughed, "I can't take breaks without feeling guilty. I did grow up in service, you know."

Keira sipped her tea as Mistress Morgan asked after Arielle's mother.

"She's doing well. The midwife said we shouldn't worry, but Mother ought to take it easy. She's coming right along."

"Very sensible. Now," Mistress Morgan set her tea down with a click, "to what do I owe the visit?"

"Keira has a unique problem and we were hoping you'd have some advice."

"Oh?" She turned her attention to Keira.

"It's not really a problem, but I could use advice." Keira hesitated.

"Well, out with it. I can't help if I don't know the details."

Keira stared into her cup for a long moment, watching the steam curl from the fragrant tea and doubting her goals. Seeing such a casual use of magic made her think it would be nice to actually learn. Ironic, considering it was the same thing that had made her devalue her gift. But...if it could be used so casually, then it must be relatively easy to control...eventually.

"Mistress Morgan, is it easy to learn magic?" She asked.

She snorted so hard that some of her dark curls flopped into her eyes. "No. And I was serious, *Selene*, if you please."

Keira grimaced apologetically. "I didn't quite mean it the way it came out. I meant is it easy to control magic — not to set your books on fire when you're trying to heat tea, for instance."

Selene took a sip of tea, eyes far away. "It is now. But I was never prone to accidents. When my magic went awry during training it was usually because it wasn't strong enough."

"What happens if your magic isn't strong enough?"

"If you let it go, nothing. It gets easier to estimate your own strength with time. Are you looking for an apprenticeship? I'm afraid I'd make a poor master, but I might be able to help you find someone better."

"No, not exactly. I-" Keira paused, struggling to find the right words.

"Quite the opposite." Arielle said with a sigh.

Mistress Selene looked to Keira with wide brown eyes, waiting for her to explain.

"Well, you see." Keira steeled herself for what she was about to say. *This is someone Arielle trusts.* "I'm a Natural. I don't want to learn, but I was hoping—"

"You don't have a choice." Selene set her cup down with a click. "I'm astonished that you managed to live so long untrained."

"What do you mean I don't have a choice?" Keira asked in alarm. Or 'managed to live so long'?

"Doesn't it pull at you?"

"Well yes, but—"

"You must learn. The sooner the better."

"I was hoping you'd have some advice for burying it."

"My dear, if you are a Natural ArKen there's nothing to be done, but once you've begun training, you may find that you like it. I certainly did."

Keira choked back her feelings. She didn't want to fall apart in front of a stranger. Her free hand curled into a fist in her skirt. She felt trapped, her throat tight and her body hot and cold at the same time. Where had the air gone? Keira couldn't speak.

"Don't look so glum. Magic can be a delight, once you find what you're good at."

"She's scared," Arielle explained.

"It isn't anything to fear, my dear." Selene patted her hand.

"Last time I tried to do magic I lit my bed on fire."

Selene sat back in surprise. "That isn't a typical problem, but Naturals are a lot more powerful than your average ArKen. I'll try to come up with a list, if you would find it useful?"

"List?"

"Of possible tutors. In the meantime, I recommend avoiding experimentation."

"That won't be a problem. Thank you, Mistress Selene."

"You aren't my apprentice. Call me Selene."

"What do you think of Master Elers?" Keira asked.

Selene shrugged. "I don't know him all that well, but I understand he's a skilled healer. It's advanced magic. He might be an option, although I don't know if he's had an apprentice before."

To Keira's surprise, the conversation turned to other topics. She supposed magic seemed less extraordinary to someone who must use it daily. Selene and Arielle chatted about the weather while they finished their tea. Selene's enthusiasm for the topic was exactly as reported. It made Keira smile, even if she was too distracted to do more than mention that she had read Selene's book and listen while the others talked.

* * *

Keira hadn't seen much of her pa recently. He was focused on his work, while she was focused on her studies. The rare mornings when she was awake early enough to see him shone like gems in her memory. On one such morning in late summer, her pa made an announcement.

"I got the commission."

"I knew you would!" Keira's mom handed her a plate of eggs and cup of juice before joining him on the couch.

He kissed his wife on the forehead and his voice took on a deeper pitch. "You're such a sweet liar."

"So you'll be crafting a present for a duke's son?" Her mom set a hand on his chest.

Keira kept her eyes on her plate of eggs, her stockinged toes digging into their bearskin rug as her mom made eyes at her pa. She cleared her throat.

Her pa laughed and pulled away. "His Grace came in person to give me the details."

"No?" Keira couldn't believe it.

"Duke Duval?"

"Of course! The next nearest duke is all the way up in Polaris."

Her mom giggled. "Well, you never know."

"Duval?" Keira nearly spilled her juice. "You aren't making something for Lord Fionn Duval, are you?"

"I am. But that's not the best part." Her pa waited until he had their full attention, puffing out his chest as he stretched the silence out for effect. When he spoke again, he sounded like one of the booming announcers at a horse race. "We've all been invited to Lord Duval's birthday celebration!"

"Attend a nobleman's party?" Keira paled. "Can we *do* that?"

Her pa chuckled and took her hand, "Sprout, we were invited. They wouldn't invite us if we weren't welcome."

Keira shrank further into the rocking chair. "Are you sure it isn't some standing custom that we should refuse? It may be a courtesy and…"

He shook his head. "I had the same thought, but the other blacksmiths have had similar invitations and felt no need to turn them down."

"It's common practice to invite the craftsmen if you commission something that will be presented at a party. Although, including his family is unusually considerate to include his family." Her mom added, beaming. "Oh darling!

Keira smoothed her dress and set her plate aside.

"And you will *both* have a new dress for the occasion." Her pa's eyes twinkled.

"No pa. I couldn't! That's an expense we don't need."

"That's my decision to make, Sprout." He gently elbowed his wife. "Besides, we both know your mom would kill me if I let you attend such a fete in an old dress. She's from the city, you know. She saw many such parties in her younger days."

Her mom's gaze grew distant as he finished. Keira had no trouble imagining her mother swirling through a ballroom among nobles and wealthy merchants. She was beautiful. Svelte, with long blonde hair, grey eyes, porcelain skin, and delicate features.

"When is the party?"

"The second day of the last month of autumn. I have plenty of time to get the blade right."

Four

Weeks seemed to slip away as Keira settled more firmly into a routine. She started every morning with a slow and contemplative session of archery. Then she breakfasted with Arielle and Dymphna. Arielle was often busy, but Keira spent each morning holed up in a corner of the library and Arielle joined her when she could. Lord Duval even joined her a few times. He never failed to tease her about her fascination with the ceiling lights, but she was certain he couldn't feel them the way that she did. Whatever force kept them aloft and prevented them from touching each other seemed to hum in her mind. Rather than find it distracting, Keira enjoyed the soft background noise. It kept her from focusing too much on her own rebellious power.

She made a point of interrupting Selene's work sometime during the day to make sure she stretched her legs and ate. Except for the list of ArKen Selene had promised, they didn't talk about magic or Keira's research, but they did discuss the natural world. Selene was an enthusiast of natural science and Keira was quickly catching her disease.

Sometime in late afternoon Keira always forced herself to stop studying and take their old mule, Cinnamon, out for a ride. He was more used to cart work, but she was glad he had been trained for both. She was careful to keep their rides short at first, but Cinnamon seemed to enjoy them as much as she did.

Keira ate supper in the dining hall, or she and Arielle would go to Dymphna's room. Usually there was a little sewing to do while the three friends chatted after dinner. Then she stayed up studying by firelight.

Keira was enjoying herself, but she was still completely lost regarding magic. She had twice tried to broach the subject with her pa, but he thought they should wait for more information and Keira was happy for an excuse to delay an intimidating conversation.

During her nightly studies, Keira indulged in more targeted reading. It was the only time she felt she could read about magic without being observed. There were still very few books on the subject available to her. Selene had helped her find a few more, tucked in odd corners of the library — the shelving of these volumes seemed to make sense to her, unless she had the whole library memorized, a feat Keira wouldn't put past her. Even with the additional material, Keira had not managed to understand anything new.

One of the last nights of summer, Keira sat alone on the floor in her family's sitting room. A gentle breeze cooled the back of her neck as she squinted at a passage in *An Introduction to the Arcane*. It described a practical application that she had been drooling over for weeks — how to create the globe lights that floated under the ceiling of the library.

The more Keira read, the more excited she became. *This sounds easy. It's so simple!* She laid the book aside, held both hands in front of herself, and took a deep breath. *Do I dare?* She looked around and took another deep breath, focusing on the warm light of the power inside herself. Her eyes flew open. When had it grown so strong? Her hands shook with momentary panic before she reined herself in. *This is not helpful.*

She closed her eyes again. Taking a full, steadying breath, she looked inward. Instead of trying to do anything with her power, she just watched it for a minute, getting used to the idea of its existence. It seemed to pulse in an unsettling way. *But that's why I'm doing this,* she told herself, *I have to learn.*

Keira kept her eyes closed and pulled a tiny thread of power to be used. She wanted to snap it off the larger piece but wasn't quite sure what the results of that would be. Instead, she focused on moving it slowly and carefully.

She held up her hands, breathed "Light!" and her eyes snapped open.

An orb light bloomed into life in her hand, yellow like the sun. Then she screamed and dropped the thread as a searing pain spread through her palms. It was so intense that she couldn't focus her eyes.

Her pa was at her side in a moment, holding her shaking arms by the wrists. "What happened?" he yelled.

"Water daddy, get the water!" She gestured at the pitcher that sat on a table, voice cracking as she cried fat tears.

He was there and back in half a moment and held it at an angle so she could stick her hands in the cool water. She cried for a long time. Her hands were red and blistered as though she had grabbed a hot pan from the oven.

"I think I conjured a piece of the sun." She finally said through a haze of tears.

She scooted the book toward her pa with her foot as she noticed her mom's arm around her shoulders for the first time. "I'm sorry. I thought I was being careful. It seemed easy and the lights in the library aren't hot." She looked down at her blistered skin and a fresh wave of tears fell.

"I'm going to get a healer. Keep your hands in the water." Her pa ordered.

She obediently put them back in the pitcher, which her mom angled in her lap so her hands could reach the water without touching the sides.

"Don't leave me," she whimpered.

"I'm here darling." Her mom kept one arm around her, and steadied the pitcher with the other.

What followed were the longest fifteen minutes of Keira's nineteen years. She had not known a person could hurt this badly. She was racked by waves of black pain as she sat there, almost unaware that her hands were hands and not simply pain incarnate. She vaguely wondered if it would hurt less if she cut them off. The room looked darker than it was, and there were still spots on her vision from the brilliance of the light she had created.

The minutes seemed to stretch on for an eternity. She was trapped, unable to move because of the pitcher in her mother's lap. Every couple of minutes a piercing cry escaped her, whenever she made the mistake of folding a hand or bending a finger. Once, the pitcher slipped an inch and her hand bumped the side. That brought on the worst scream, and she did not stop blubbering until she heard her pa returning with help.

Declan Elers was with him. It was shocking that he was the only one, given the racket she had been making, but castle walls were thicker than those she was used to. Keira pulled her hands from the pitcher to show him and he rushed to kneel on the floor beside her.

"How did this happen?" He demanded, grabbing her shaking wrists.

She shook her head. It was too long an explanation to squeeze through her tears.

"I need to know. It will help with the healing," he said tightly.

Her pa grabbed the magic book and handed it to Elers. "She was trying to make a light."

"It's a different page." Keira said through a hoarse throat.

His brown eyes grew wide. "This is why I told you to speak with me if you wanted to learn."

Keira had no answer except more tears. Her burned hands throbbed even worse outside of the water.

"I cannot heal this in one session, but I'll do what I can tonight."

He gently turned her wrists so her palms faced upward and placed his hands under hers. Closing his eyes, he drew several slow breaths while Keira sat as still as she could manage. It was the oddest sensation. For a moment, her pain dulled, then she felt a foreign power sinking into her hands. They throbbed and the power dissipated.

"What are you doing?" Master Elers growled, "Let me heal you."

"I stopped you?" She asked in surprise.

"Yes." His eyes snapped open. "You weren't aware of it?"

She shook her head, tears stinging her eyes as the pain returned to her hands.

"How is that possible?" He released her hands.

Keira let them rest palm up in her lap but flinched when a small motion pulled at the blistered skin. "I'm a Natural."

Elers blinked. "An untrained Natural?"

She nodded again.

"Well small wonder you couldn't resist." He shook his head. "Okay, I'm going to need you to focus. Can you feel your power?"

"Always."

He nodded, "Right then…." He sat back and crossed his legs.

Keira shifted and another yelp escaped her.

"Can you focus through the pain? Take a deep breath. Most people sense their magic as a glowing sphere occupying the center of their mind. Is that what it looks like to you?"

Keira shook her head. "Sometimes, but usually it seems more like my whole mind is glowing." She laughed nervously.

"That's good!" He exclaimed. "I think it will help you understand this."

"I can't focus. Can you do that one more time? It helped for a minute." Keira held her hands up.

"It's not exactly a comfortable feeling to have your power ripped to shreds."

"Did I hurt you?" Keira stuck her hands back in the water instead.

"Not exactly, but it used up some of my strength. The more I can conserve right now, the better."

Keira nodded her understanding, "I'll do my best then."

"Our instinctive perception of our power is wrong." Elers began, "Or at least incomplete. It exists in our mind, but also in our bodies. See if you can feel it."

Keira closed her eyes and tried. She *really* tried, but after a minute she shook her head.

"What did it feel like when I tried to heal you?"

Keira thought back. It was harder than it should have been. The pain of her burns made her mind feel foggy. The corners of her vision still seemed darker than they should be and tears leaked steadily down her cheeks, but she tried to ignore it.

"At first, it just dulled the pain."

"Really?" Elers interrupted. "I hadn't done anything yet."

Keira shrugged, "It dulled the pain." She insisted, "Then I felt your power sink into my hands. And they sort of throbbed. Then it was gone."

"The human body cannot detect magic. What you felt was my power intersecting with yours."

Keira tried to absorb this new information. "Let me try again."

She closed her eyes. After a few deep breaths she was able to feel something other than the pain in her hands. An awareness of her body, and the image of herself as a glowing figure filled her mind.

"Oh." Was all she said.

"You feel it?" Master Elers asked.

She nodded.

He positioned their hands as he had before and closed his eyes. "Stay aware of that and...keep it calm."

She felt the dulling of her pain again and closed her eyes in relief. This time when the foreign magic slipped through hers she held very still on more than a physical level. It soon felt like cool water had been poured into her, filling her hands completely. But her power ran away from her.

This time, instead of destroying the invading magic, it amplified it. She felt herself following Elers' reach with her own and her power flowed into his. She did not direct it. It wanted to act, but she held back. Keira did not have the knowledge necessary to treat a burn. Elers was restoring a web of white threads that ran under her skin. Her hands tingled as he worked, but the pain diminished continually.

She breathed a sigh of relief. "Thank you."

He continued working for a few minutes, then withdrew his hands. "I have done all I can for now. It was more than I would have believed possible. You helped."

She opened her eyes to find the skin unchanged.

"But...you didn't do anything." Her pa said from his position above the pair.

"He did." Keira sighed. "The pain is gone."

"I don't know about that. It's diminished; the nerves are repaired, which I never could have accomplished so quickly on my own. I have dampened them for now, but that effect will not last more than twelve hours." He opened the bag he carried and began rummaging through it.

"So that's what those white threads were?" Keira asked. "It feels like you threw a cold wet towel over them."

Elers laughed, "Interesting description. I've never worked on someone so aware of my progress — or so helpful. It's a good thing you didn't try to do anything on your own though. You could have done a lot of damage."

"I guessed that. It seemed like delicate work...and my last experiment wasn't exactly successful."

"Healing is delicate." He pulled out clean bandages and a jar of some sort of green ointment.

Next, Elers found a soft cloth, a waterskin, and a bottle of clear viscous fluid. He ever so gently washed her hands, but Keira still flinched at the touch of the towel. She made herself stay quiet with a massive effort. When that was done, he applied the ointment, which felt lovely cool on her damaged skin and the open spot at the base of her thumbs. Finally, he covered her palms and fingers in a strange porous bandage and wrapped the entirety of her hands in linen.

"Do not get these wet." He ordered firmly, meeting her green eyes with his gray. He ran a hand through his dark hair, "Don't use them at all if you can help it. The blisters will help it heal some if you don't break them."

"Yes, Master Elers. Thank you." Keira found her feet with his help.

"I am not 'Master'. You are an ArKen and entitled to call me Declan, as my friends do."

His face didn't reveal any emotion. He did look a little pinched around the eyes, and almost green in the darkness. She vaguely wondered if he was nauseous.

"Thank you, De-Declan." Keira stammered.

"Oh." He handed her pa several packets. "She may have a tea brewed with one of these every eight hours for pain. She will need it, so don't wait for it to start hurting."

"I'll make sure she gets it. Thank you."

"Come see me tomorrow afternoon and I'll work on your injury again."

"How much do I owe you?" Keira's pa took a step toward the mantle, where his purse sat.

"Nothing. I'm in the king's employ and serve those residing in the castle."

He bowed and Keira gave a little bob, since she couldn't grab her skirt to curtsy. Her mom gave a proper one while her pa returned the bow. Then Master Elers was gone.

"I need to be trained." Keira said into the dark room.

"Keira." Her parents said in unison.

She shook her head. "I have to."

A long silence followed, during which her parents shared a

communicative look. When she was starting to think they wouldn't answer, her pa spoke.

"We won't stop you Sprout, just...be careful."

"I swear."

* * *

The following day was rough for Keira. She had grown used to her routine, and breaking it was almost more painful than her burned hands. *Almost.* She couldn't do any of the things that normally occupied her time. Her bow sat useless in her bedroom, and there was no way she would be able to ride. She couldn't even read. Turning pages proved a monumental task. It was frustrating, but she was grateful that her magic seemed content to slumber — whether because she had unleashed it or because she was distracted by the pain, Keira couldn't have said.

Eventually, she gave up on her normal pursuits and went in search of some company. She found Arielle reshelving books in the library. Her friend was horrified when she learned what had happened, although Keira spared her some of the gruesome details. Arielle immediately demanded a promise not to try any more magic without a teacher. It was an easy thing to give. Keira wasn't exactly eager to make another attempt.

"I'm supposed to go see Master Elers this afternoon so he can work on them some more." Keira took a deep breath and let it out with a sigh. "And I'm going to ask him about teaching me."

"After this?" Arielle asked, startled.

"Yes. Arielle. You don't understand — I watched him heal me. I *helped*!"

"This is big." Did you talk to your parents?"

"A little. I have their permission, if not their approval. But I have to admit I'm nervous."

"Sure, who wouldn't be? Magic is wonderful, but only a fool would be completely comfortable learning it." She paused before grasping her uninjured forearm. "Oh, Keira! I'm so happy for you."

Keira blushed. "Master Elers is so...intimidating."

"I know. I think it's because he's so tall." Arielle laughed. She fiddled with her long braid as she shelved a few more books from her cart. "And he walks around with a blank expression all day. I believe he's just lost in thought, but it does sometimes look like he's angry."

"Ah yes, resting dragon face." Keira grinned. "He must be a water dragon though. He's an amazing healer."

"I'm glad he could help you. Burns can be really bad if they're deep."

"I know." Keira sighed.

"How bad was it?" Arielle asked with sudden suspicion.

"It was a severe second degree burn, based on what I've read." Keira hedged, itching the back of one hand with the back of the other.

"That must be painful." Arielle's face softened in sympathy and she squeezed her shoulder.

"It was. It isn't too bad today if I don't touch anything."

"How did you eat breakfast? I didn't see you in the dining hall."

"I skipped it."

Arielle set her pile of books on her hip and gave her a hard look. "No. You need to eat to heal."

Keira shrugged, "I'm not hungry. The tea Master Elers gave me for pain makes my stomach hurt."

"It wouldn't if you ate something. Come on." Arielle looped one arm through Keira's and dropped the rest of the books at the front desk.

Arielle marched her to her own rooms. It was Keira's first time seeing them and somehow, it had never occurred to her that Arielle would have her own suite. It was several doors down and around a corner from her parents'.

A copper brazier stood on one end of the sitting room, next to a heavy wooden desk. The apartment was interior, so there were no windows, but curtains divided the living room from the hall. They were dyed a deep blue with little yellow flowers. On closer inspection, Keira realized they were woven that way.

"We brought those from our homeland." Arielle explained, and when Keira looked puzzled she added, "The Southern Isles. It isn't really another kingdom, but it sure feels like it."

"How so?"

"Everything's different. The Isles have the same king, of course — but the weather, the food, and the fashions are different."

"Was it hotter?"

"And humid." Arielle confirmed, "So the clothes are lighter, and they have brighter dyes. Some crazy plants grow there."

Arielle pulled down a book from a shelf near the desk and flipped it open. "This one's my favorite."

She pulled a pressed flower in the brightest orange Keira had ever seen from between two pages. It looked gaudy as nature never did. She refrained from saying so, however. If this was Arielle's favorite flower then she would try to appreciate it. Perhaps it looked better fresh?

"Make yourself comfortable." Arielle gestured at the padded armchairs that adorned her sitting room. "I'm going to make us some tea."

Keira sat on a yellow cushion and looked down at the ornate rug under her feet. It was woven in an impossibly intricate pattern, bright colors warring with each other for attention. The main contenders seemed to be orange, yellow, and a blue that was almost black. Or was it purple? Keira was confused for a moment until she realized it started as blue at one end of the rug and became almost a red at the other. It was an assault on her senses, but she couldn't look away.

It was only a few minutes until Arielle joined her, laying a tray of tea and snack cakes on the table beside Keira. Arielle drew another chair close and placed a slice of hearty looking bread on a small plate. She cut it with a fork and held it out for Keira.

"Thank you." Keira felt incredibly awkward as she accepted the bite.

Arielle continued to tell her about her first home as if feeding her was just a routine part of their relationship. She fed Keira another slice of the nut-heavy bread and helped her drink a cup of tea while they talked.

"Thank you." Keira said afterward, shifting uncomfortably. "You made that a lot less awkward than I expected it to be."

Arielle shook her head, "I used to do that all the time for my grandmother. It wasn't awkward for me."

Keira was too embarrassed to be fed in the dining hall, so the pair had lunch in Keira's rooms. Dymphna joined them and completely ignored the fact that Arielle was feeding their friend, except to ask what had happened to her hands. When Keira explained, she went pale.

"I guess magic is more dangerous than I realized. I didn't know ArKen could hurt themselves too." Dymphna admitted, graciously refraining from commenting on the news that her friend apparently was one.

"I don't think it's that common, but I could have told you magic was dangerous. I set my bed on fire once."

"You did what?" Dymphna dropped the spoon she was holding.

"I....set my bed on fire. I was trying to light a candle." Keira shrugged. "Yesterday was the first time I've tried magic since. It sort of....seeps out occasionally, but nothing bad has ever happened from that."

"Seeps...out...." Even her freckles looked pale.

"Yeah....but it hasn't done that for years." Keira tried to reassure her friend. "I've been more careful."

"That probably happens to all Naturals." Arielle said after a long pause, "But you're the first one I've met."

Keira laughed. "Are we that uncommon?"

"Yes." Her friends said in unison.

Keira blinked. She knew more than one. Her Aunt Rose had brought a friend with her on more than one visit when she was little. She could probably name four other Naturals. She doubted she would recognize them if she saw them again, however.

"I never realized because it runs in my family." She finally admitted, looking down at her bandaged hands.

"Runs in your family?" Dymphna sounded like she was struggling to get her words out, or possibly to get her breath in.

Keira felt her heart twist. Her new friend had mentioned that she was afraid of magic before, and now she joined them for this. She felt a little sick, and she didn't think it was her tea. Would Dymphna avoid her from now on?

"Her Aunt is a Natural as well." Arielle explained.

"Why didn't she train you?" Dymphna's pale eyebrows knit together.

"Papa didn't want me to learn."

"Why?" Dymphna asked, eyebrows flying into her hairline.

Keira shrugged. "Recently he told me he doesn't want me to be alone. I think he just loves my mom so much he thinks that marriage is how you find joy."

"That's actually really sweet," Arielle said, smiling dreamily.

"It's adorable, if you ask me," Dymphna added with a goofy grin of her own.

Keira couldn't help smiling too. "Yeah. I suppose it is. I think I'd like marrying. I always planned on it, but learning magic doesn't necessarily mean I won't get the chance."

"You'll have a copper's chance in a gambler's pocket," Dymphna said bluntly.

"Maybe." Keira sighed, "I don't really have a choice anymore though. I've learned that Naturals never do."

They chatted amongst themselves for a few more minutes.

"Well, I've a lot of chores to do today," Dymphna finally said, standing with a long-suffering sigh. "Duchess Duval is having some guests. I probably won't be around tomorrow either."

Keira couldn't help but wonder if that had more to do with her magic than Duchess Duval's guests, but she tried to hide her worry. "That's alright. I'm headed to see Master Elers. He just said 'this afternoon', but I don't see the point of waiting. It is after noon now."

"Do you need some company?" Arielle asked.

"No..I'll be alright." Keira straightened her shoulders. "I can handle it. Unless he asks me to call him Declan again."

"Declan?' The others chorused.

"Yes." Keira groaned, "He said ArKen don't refer to each other as master. But....he's a noble. How am I just supposed to call him Declan?"

"It sounds to me as if he's a good candidate for teacher. You should definitely ask him today," Arielle encouraged her.

"So...you're really planning to learn, then? Soon?" Dymphna asked.

"She'll have to."

"That's my intention." Keira stood. "Well, better sooner than later. I guess I'll see you at dinner."

Five

Keira fretted all the way to the first floor, then realized she didn't actually know where Master Elers' office was. She wandered around trying to find another person to ask, but there were no people in the corridors this time of day. There weren't even any servants running errands for a noble. Eventually, she turned around, planning to go back and ask her friends. As she did, she smacked right into Lord Duval. He was dressed casually, the only hint of his wealth a chunky silver ring that looked like it might have a crest on it.

"Pardon me, milord." Keira immediately sank into a curtsy.

"I was walking too close." He chuckled. "I was trying to ask — are you looking for something?'

"Master Elers' office."

"As it happens, I'm on my way there. Join me?" He grinned and offered his arm as if she was a lady.

Keira bobbed a small curtsy. "Thank you, milord."

A little late, she accepted his arm. It felt awkward, since she was unable to rest her hand on the inside of his arm. She fought to hide how much her hands wanted to tremble.

When he broke the awkward silence, she was glad he didn't ask about her bandages. "Have you read anything good lately?"

Keira nodded and started rambling about a volume of short stories she had found in the library. Most of them had some sort of unexpected twist that left her laughing. Lord Duval had already read it and laughed along with her as they compared their favorites.

Before Keira could believe it, they were standing outside a wooden door with a silver symbol painted across the top half. Three interlocked circles with a bead at different locations around the rings. She touched it with her bandaged fingertips, curious about its meaning.

Lord Duval opened the door without knocking and led Keira in with a hand on her back. It was a fascinating room. Two rooms, actually. The first was furnished almost like a sitting room, if you were used to large gatherings. There was a cornflower blue rug that nearly reached each wall. Several padded chairs sat along the edges with flimsy end tables between them. The tables were piled with leaflets and a few worn books. This left the center of the room open for foot traffic. Keira glanced at the ceiling, which boasted several of the heatless orbs of light that illuminated the library. These were blue and green. They lent the empty sitting area a relaxing atmosphere.

Lord Duval led her straight through the first room and into the second through an open door. Master Elers sat at a oversized birchwood desk. Its surface was pristine, even the piled papers to one side seemed almost miraculously straight and even.

Two armchairs sat on the opposite side of the desk, and Lord Duval seated himself in one of those. The rest of the office was occupied by bookshelves filled to their precise capacity and a large couch that sat facing a cushioned stool.

"Declan, I brought you a client." Lord Duval leaned back and picked one leg up to set it on the desk.

This earned him an icy glare from Master Elers.

He only laughed. "Loosen up. This is why people find you intimidating."

Keira looked down at her bandaged hands.

"Miss Smith! Please, have a seat."

She sat, trying to smooth out her skirt before she remembered it would hurt. She took a deep, steadying breath.

"Are you ready for another round of healing?" Master Elers asked, reaching across the desk.

"Yes please, milord." Keira held her hands out, palms turned upward.

"Do you object to Lord Duval's presence?" He asked gently.

Keira shook her head. Master Elers unwrapped her bandages with slow care, but Keira still had to grit her teeth against the pain as they caught in wet spots. The skin didn't look much worse than it had the night before, except that she could see it better in the light. She fought back a wave of nausea.

Lord Duval hissed through his teeth and covered his mouth with a fist.

She focused her attention on Master Elers. "Can I help like I did before?"

"Yes. But don't forget what happened on our first attempt."

"Right." Keira closed her eyes and took several slow breaths until she was aware of her magic throughout her body.

"Let me know when you're ready to begin." Elers said smoothly, placing his palms under her hands.

"I'm ready." Her eyes fluttered open.

He closed his own and began. She followed with her mind. This time, they worked closer to the surface. Keira was surprised to find that healthy skin seemed to be made of little pancake-shaped bubbles stacked on top of each other. She was alarmed by how few of these had survived on the palm side of her hands.

"What are those pancakes?" She asked, unable to stop herself.

"Pancakes?" Lord Duval laughed.

"I'm guessing you mean cells. Please save questions for after we've finished. I need to focus."

"I'm sorry," Keira said, abashed.

Master Elers worked with what she had. Keira watched in amazement as he coaxed her healthy cells to divide and grow. She added her power to his and before long her fingers no longer felt tight and painful. She sneaked a peek and found the palms were unmarred by any sign of her burn. They hadn't even scarred.

She found Lord Duval watching in fascination. She met his amber eyes before closing her own again. Master Elers was pulling tiredly at the stubborn area near her left thumb. She buoyed his strength with her own and the open spot on each hand was quickly addressed. It seemed a long time before they were finished. Keira's shoulders started to ache from holding her arms up, but Elers ignored their shared fatigue.

When they both finally opened their eyes, Keira's skin was smooth and unbroken. There was no sign left of her injury, but she was exhausted. She could tell from the way Elers' face slumped that he was at least as tired as she was.

"Thank you," she breathed.

"I'm glad you were able to help me," he answered with a heavy sigh. "This would have taken at least a week to heal without your assistance."

"But I saw you heal a broken leg in an hour!" Keira exclaimed.

"You did what?" Lord Duval asked.

The healer chuckled. "It was a minor fracture. A large bone, but I only hurried along the natural process of healing. This injury was different."

"How so?" Keira asked, her natural curiosity restored now that the pain was gone.

She flexed her hands, rubbing her fingers gently over the smooth skin on her palm while she waited for his answer. She had expected to be permanently disfigured at the very least, and she was so grateful that she seemed to have regained their full use that she felt tears building behind her eyes.

"Your burns would have left you with limited use of your hands if left to heal naturally." He explained, in a matter-of-fact tone. "The muscles were unaffected, but you had severe nerve damage. Nerves do not heal without magical assistance."

Keira nodded. She had read as much in one of the many

medical texts she had devoured since moving to the castle. It made sense then that it had taken so much effort from both of them.

"Your skin would not have healed either," he continued in the same, almost harsh tone. "There was none left on much of your palms. You would have been left with thick, granulated scar tissue. It would have been difficult to close and open your hands."

Now she did cry. Keira could not help the tears that flowed. "Thank you, Master Elers."

Lord Duval put an arm around her shoulders. "A little much, don't you think."

"No. She needs to know the consequences of what she did." Elers replied, unmoved.

"Did?"

"He's right. That's not why I'm crying." Keira wiped her eyes with her unblemished fingers, trying to regain control. "I just really missed my hands."

"But what did you do?" Lord Duval asked, still confused.

"She tried magic unsupervised and injured herself."

He dropped his arm. "Why would you do that? Everyone knows you need an instructor to learn magic."

Keira shrugged.

"Do you have one?" Master Elers asked.

"Not yet milord. I was hoping to ask you about that today." Keira's heart raced at her own boldness, and she had to fight to keep her back straight.

"Enough with the 'milord'."

"Yes, Master Elers." She gave a wan smile.

Lord Duval chuckled.

"There are very few who could fulfill the office for an untrained Natural at your age." Elers said, ignoring the pair of them.

"Could you?" Keira asked, pressing the palms of her newly healed hands flat against her stomach.

"Yes, I believe so." He pursed his lips. "We would have to take certain precautions. Most masters are stronger than their pupils and can subvert their mistakes. You would be especially dangerous, given the interest you have expressed in healing."

"Will you teach me?" Keira asked after a long silence.

"Do you still want to be a healer?" He asked.

"Yes — more than ever," she said quickly, looking down at her hands. "But...I haven't gotten my papa's permission."

"His permission is irrelevant. It isn't safe for you to remain untrained. The consequences could be devastating, and not just for you."

"Is it possible to seal my magic away?"

"Some theorize it is, but no one has ever survived the attempt."

"Oh." Keira looked down, and couldn't help the rebellious smile that tugged at her lips. "Then I suppose I must apply myself to the study of magic."

"I'll teach you. But you need to understand that learning magic can be a years' long process. Are you prepared for the commitment? If your training is left incomplete, you could be more dangerous than when we started."

"I'm fully committed, Master Elers."

"If we're going to be working together for years you had better just call me Declan."

"Yes, Master Declan."

Lord Duval laughed. "I'm going to like having you around." He said easily.

She blushed but couldn't keep a grin from her face.

"Will you call me Fionn?" he asked. "We'll be seeing a lot of each other, I'm sure."

"I will. Thank you Fionn."

"Why so easily?" Her new master complained.

Keira couldn't explain. Elers was so...serious? Accomplished? *Scary*. She finally decided.

"We'll begin your instruction right now. How did this happen, exactly?" He was all business.

"Well, I was reading *An Introduction to the Arcane*, and I

found a passage that seemed to be a bit more practical. It sounded simple enough and I at least knew what the result should look like since I spend so much time in the library."

"You attempted to make one of these?" Elers held out his hand and one of the orbs in the next room flew to it.

"Yes, exactly." Keira nodded. "I was so careful. I know my magic is strong, so I just grabbed one thread to work with. I thought I had it under control."

"I'm pleased instinct told you as much. How did it get away from you?"

"It didn't. But when I made the light it was hot. I think I was holding a piece of the sun."

"If you were holding a piece of the sun, you'd be dead." He grimaced. "My guess is that when you think about light, you unconsciously connect it with heat."

"It never occurred to me that the two were separate," Keira admitted.

"They can be." Elers smiled. "Good. It was a problem of understanding rather than control. That's easier to fix."

"I have to admit. I'm not eager to try that again." Keira leaned against the back of her chair, shuddering at the memory.

"No, that won't be the first thing you learn. First, I need an idea of your background knowledge. Do you have anything you need to do this afternoon?"

"Nothing pressing."

"Good. We may be interrupted if there are injuries, but my schedule is otherwise empty."

Fionn excused himself, and Keira spent the majority of that afternoon with Master Elers. After Fionn was gone, it seemed like Elers' lukewarm exterior froze over. He had a thousand questions for Keira and it didn't seem like he was pleased with her answers.

Many of the questions seemed to repeat themselves, but Elers forced her to expand on her answers until she was guessing. It seemed that some of the books she had been reading were very old, so a piece of her medical knowledge was outdated. Her master assured her that the newer understandings were built on the old.

"It's still a reasonable starting place, as long as we're careful to correct any misconceptions you may have picked up."

Eventually, he ran out of questions. Keira looked up in confusion when the barrage stopped. Elers' forehead furrowed. *Is he angry?* She was certain she must have disappointed him. *What if he decides I'm not worth teaching?* His warning about the danger her magic posed echoed through her mind. He waited so long to speak again that she could feel her heart speeding up.

At length, he stretched. "Well, I think I've gotten an idea of your knowledge base."

"My family only moved to Ravenstone Keep two and a half months ago." Keira explained, embarrassed. "I like reading, but there weren't a lot of books available back in Stoneybrooke."

He tilted his head. "You can't have absorbed so much medical knowledge in that time."

"I was planning to be a midwife. I'd been shadowing our village midwife Althea for a few months. I thought she was a good teacher." Keira blushed when she realized she had implied that she herself knew a lot.

"She must have been. I'm surprised you didn't stay to complete your apprenticeship."

Keira looked down at her hands, folded tightly in her lap. "Papa thought it best we stay together, given my secret...and since I'm not married. It was never an official apprenticeship."

"Well, he was probably right." Elers shrugged and pulled out a smooth sheet of parchment. "I'll schedule a meeting with the king's chancellor, to make this official."

"The chancellor?" Keira's eyes widened. She didn't know who that was, but they sounded important.

"Yes, since I serve the crown it will be necessary to get permission to take on an apprentice."

"Oh." Keira bit her lip.

"There's no reason we should be denied. It's just a matter of paperwork. Is there any time that would be convenient for you?"

"Whatever time works for you, Master El-Declan." She bit her lip again.

His eyes crinkled with the first smile she had seen in hours. "I'll see how soon he can squeeze us in. Try to get some rest for the next couple of days. Your body could use it after all that healing."

Feeling herself to be dismissed, Keira rose and curtsied. She waited for him to say anything else, but he just nodded and bent to write a letter. Keira awkwardly edged out of the room.

Well, no time like the present, she told herself. *I must talk to Pa.*

* * *

When she left Master Declan's office, it was late afternoon. Keira felt too tired to settle into any serious activity, but she knew she needed to speak with her pa about her apprenticeship. With a sigh, she headed in that direction.

Ravenstone Keep's smithy wasn't really a building. It consisted of one stone wall abutting the castle itself and a sturdy roof supported by wooden beams. The roof was strong enough to guard against inclement weather and there were treated canvas sides that could be rolled down if the need arose.

The open-sided structure provided a relatively cool working environment for the smiths. It supported one massive forge and six smaller forges inside. There was room for as many as twelve smiths to work safely together inside, though there were only seven that day. There were three such buildings clustered at the back of the castle and one close to the city gate.

Keira's papa worked with the other specialized weapon smiths at the forge closest to the castle entrance. She found him hard at work, massive forearms bared as he hammered on the formless steel that would learn the shape of a blade under his hand. *I wonder if that's for Fionn.*

"Keira!" Her papa set a heavy hammer aside and shoved the flattened steel back into the coals. He wiped his hands on his thick leather apron. "Let's see them."

"See what?"

He held his hands up and wiggled his soot-covered fingers.

"Oh. All better, Pa." She mimicked him.

He sagged with relief and murmured half to himself, "Not even a mark."

"Master Elers was thorough." She agreed with a smile, but it faded quickly. "Papa?"

"Yes?" He moved the steel to a different part of the fire, watching it closely.

"I need to talk to you about something."

He waited expectantly.

Keira showed her teeth in a guilty grimace that she tried to turn into a smile. "I found an apprenticeship this afternoon."

"You did?" Her papa looked up from the forge with a smile.

Keira showed him her unblemished hands. "When I went to Master Elers for my second healing he asked if I had an instructor. One thing led to another, and he agreed to teach me. I said I needed to talk to you first, but he said it isn't safe. I *must* learn."

His smile disappeared, but to her surprise, he only nodded. "Your mom and I had a long talk this morning. We can't justify keeping you from training any longer, not when we've seen the consequences." His eyes grew suspiciously red and glossy.

"Oh no — Pa...that wasn't...I made a bad decision, but it *was* a choice that I made. Please don't blame yourself for what happened to my hands."

"I'll blame myself for whatever I like. That's a father's privilege. Just you promise to be careful while you're learning."

"Of course Pa. And Master Elers seems like the cautious type."

"Master Elers — you'll be learning from the healer?"

"Yes."

"And you're alright with that?" He scratched his beard with one hand. "He does seem a bit..."

"Reserved," Keira supplied with a crooked grin. "I'll be fine Pa."

"We'll have to call you Mistress from now on," he teased.

Keira stuck her tongue out.

"What lovely manners, Mistress Sprout." He leaned in to give her a sooty hug.

"I get the feeling I won't earn that title for many years. I'm in for a long apprenticeship."

Keira was reluctant to leave. She stood off to the side and watched her papa work. It soon became clear that he was not working on the dagger for Lord Duval. Whatever he was doing seemed to be a strange curved blade with a long tang.

"I'll have to arrange a meeting with the chancellor." Her pa raised his voice to reach her above the hammering and roar of the forge. "An ArKen training in the castle could be taken the wrong way..."

"Master Elers is taking care of that. He said to rest for a couple of days and he'd arrange it as soon as possible."

Her father paused, a wistful look on his face. "That's good then."

"I have to admit, I'm nervous."

"Your mom has been asking around since you..." He swallowed. "The chancellor has a kind reputation. Just mind your manners and you'll be fine."

"I hope so." Keira looked across the castle grounds. The nearest portcullis was open and she could see through it and into the meadow beyond. The yellowed grass was dotted with purple, white, and yellow wildflowers. The golden light of late afternoon was giving way to rosy shadows, deeper beneath the gate. When had it gotten so late?

"I need to finish this up, but you should get dinner. Eat some meat tonight."

"Alright Pa." She stood on her tiptoes to kiss his cheek. "We'll make sure to have something ready for you when you've finished."

* * *

The next afternoon, Keira found herself in a dress fitting. It seemed that her pa had been serious when he said she would have a dress for the Duval's party. As much as she wanted to object to the expense, she couldn't help smiling at the gift.

The aging seamstress somehow avoided pricking her with the long pins, despite Keira's constant fidgeting. She tried to hold still, but she was simply too ticklish for such treatment. Throughout the ordeal, her mother and Arielle stood a few feet away, laughing at her.

Between adjustments, Keira ran a hand down the soft pink fabric. It was a beautiful muslin and she could hardly believe such a luxurious fabric was an option for her. The bodice would nearly match, only a shade or two darker.

She had been shocked to see the bit of lace that would be sewn at the top. It wasn't new, of course. A blacksmith could never afford new lace, but it was a treat she could not have anticipated. Still perfectly white, and only a little frayed on one edge, Keira doubted any damage would show once it was part of the dress. The seamstress had clever hands. They even ceased to tickle as she got used to Keira's jerky startling.

"It's going to be a beautiful gown," Arielle breathed as Madame Morrison added a final pin to the sleeve.

"It will be rather simple, I'm afraid," the seamstress contested.

"It doesn't seem simple to me. But if it is, that doesn't mean it won't be beautiful." Keira smiled at her, fingertips still stroking the fabric.

"Thank you for seeing us so soon," her mom added.

"Not at all dearie." The older woman patted Keira's smooth hand with her lined palm. "I'm always happy to make up something for a young lady who doesn't demand a thousand frills and stands still without complaint."

"I haven't stood *very* still." Keira chortled.

"Still enough." Madame Morrison winked. "You tried at least. That counts for something."

"It will really be done in time for the party?" Keira asked as the others helped her disengage from what had become a luxurious pricker bush.

"Six weeks is plenty of time, don't you worry. As I said, it's rather simple. Not like the other one I'm working on." She gestured at a garish yellow pile in the corner with a disapproving 'tskst'.

Keira's eyes widened at the sheer volume of fabric.

"Oh my," she and Arielle chorused.

"I see volume is still in." Her mom said with an amused quirk of her lips.

"Back in and worse than ever, I'm afraid. Now get you gone. I have work to do." The seamstress gave a toothy grin.

After giving her mom a tight hug, Keira bounded down the hall after Arielle at a less than dignified pace, eager to find Dymphna so they could discuss the party. Dymphna was ladies' maid to Duchess Duval, after all.

Six

Keira rolled out of bed and glanced outside to find a nearly black sky. She groaned as thunder rumbled through the stone floor under her bare feet. *No archery this morning.* She shivered as she kicked the blankets aside and hurried to dress in something warm.

The moment she stepped into the sitting room, her mom handed her a steaming cup of tea. It smelled heavenly. It seemed to be orange blossom and some other citrus flavor that Keira couldn't name. She curled her feet under herself on the couch and took a sip. It tasted so good that it was almost worth the burn her lack of patience had cost. She rolled her tongue and breathed through it, trying to sooth the pain away.

"A messenger brought a letter for you a little while ago. I've been resisting opening it, but I was about to wake you up. It looks rather official." Her mom handed her a rolled piece of parchment with a wax seal.

Keira set her tea aside and broke it open, burning with curiosity. It was from Master Elers; they had been granted a morning appointment with the king's chancellor. Keira couldn't help but be impressed that he could get a meeting after only a few days. She looked at the crack in their curtains. She had no idea what time it was. She handed the document to her mom.

"So soon?" She asked, eyes scanning the page. "You have to be there in an hour."

Keira's eyes widened in shock. *What would have happened if I missed an appointment with the king's chancellor?* He was one of the most important people in the government. She shivered as her fingers and toes went numb. "Will you come with me?"

Her mom's eyes scanned the note again. "I'm not invited, honey."

Keira felt cold settle in her chest. Her frozen lungs didn't want to expand.

"You'll be alright, darling. It sounds like Master Elers will be with you. But you should eat something before you go." Her mom stood and sliced her some bread.

Her mom stepped behind the couch and did her hair while Keira ate, reminding her of when she was little. Her scalp tingled while her mom combed and braided. Keira wanted to make conversation, but her mouth was too dry. She wouldn't have been able to eat even the light breakfast without washing it down with her tea. The food seemed to settle in a hard knot in her stomach.

"All done." Her mom patted her hair and pulled her to a mirror to see the twin braids.

Keira set off for the meeting, unsure where precisely the chancellor's office was. A helpful maid was able to give her some clear directions, so she made it in plenty of time. Keira found Master Elers already standing in the hall. He greeted her with a nod and she crossed the hall to stand beside him, against the wall so that they wouldn't block the corridor.

It was strange to stand without her parents, waiting for such an important meeting. When Master Elers had mentioned meeting the chancellor, she hadn't thought about it. Now, she seemed to be losing a battle with her nerves. Keira smoothed her simple green skirt with sweaty palms. She chewed on her lower lip, fighting the urge to pace. Before she knew it, she held a bundle of the thick cloth in her right hand and had to smooth it out once again.

Master Elers seemed to have no such problem. He leaned with one foot on the wall behind him. His narrow frame made him seem even taller than he was. She couldn't decide if he seemed grumpy or just sleepy, but either way it did nothing to calm her roiling nerves.

A pair of guards stood outside the door, watching them. Keira noticed that their eyes seemed trained on her. She took a deep breath to steady herself and tried to stand still. Her nervous fingers found the edge of her leather vest and she tugged it down, all too aware that the matching leather of her boots was scuffed. She felt out of place. She was fiddling with her mousy hair in its twin braids when they opened the door.

"Elers and Smith!" A papery voice called.

She rested her shaking hand on her stomach for a moment, then forced it to her side as she followed Master Elers into the room. Elers paused for only a moment and Keira stopped near the entrance to curtsy to the elderly chancellor.

His office was cramped. The room was large enough, but the desk was surrounded by walnut shelves filled with books and rolls of parchment. The desk itself was laden with a large book over which the chancellor hovered with a wet quill.

The chancellor looked up from his writing and smiled, peering through an undersized pair of spectacles. His face was relatively smooth despite his age. She stayed where she was, waiting for some instruction.

"Come in child, no need to be shy. Have a seat, both of you." He gestured at the padded chair across from him, the full sleeves of his burgundy robe almost trailing in his uncorked ink. He stopped the gesture just short of disaster, apparently aware of the danger.

"Thank you, Chancellor." She curtsied again and sat beside her new master, carefully smoothing her skirt to hide her scuffed boots.

"My schedule says you are here about seeking magical training?"

Master Elers said nothing, forcing Keira to speak.

"Y-yes." She glanced at Elers, who was mid-yawn.

The chancellor gave her a reassuring smile. "Am I to take it that you hope to study under Master Elers?"

"Yes sir."

"Magical studies are a hard road, my dear. Are you certain?"

She didn't answer immediately, and he continued.

"There is no rule against it, of course. Anyone can become a Seeker."

The chancellor moved his book aside and capped the ink bottle slowly. Keira waited, feeling awkward. She folded her hands, then unfolded them. They worked their way into her skirt, and she took a deep breath, focused on keeping her magic from showing in her eyes.

"Do you know why I had you meet me without your parents present?"

"No sir."

She looked to Elers, but he only gave a slight jerk of his head, directing her back to the chancellor.

"You're a polite one. It makes a nice change from my last meeting." The chancellor leaned forward, smiling in a grandfatherly way as he peered at her through his tiny glasses. He gave her a penetrating look. "I want to ensure that this is really what you want."

"I don't understand, chancellor." Keira licked her lips.

He sighed heavily. "Having an ArKen in the family grants a certain kind of social distinction. But that is a heavy thing to require of one's offspring. If your parents are forcing you to take this path, you have recourse my dear. If nothing else, I could help you find a husband to take you out of their power, or a position as a ladies' maid. You would answer to your Lady then."

"Oh." She gripped the edges of the chair with white hands and shook her head. "You misunderstand sir. I'm a Natural."

He leaned back in his chair, loose robes almost swallowing his thin figure. The chancellor stared at her for what felt like a long time. "A Natural? Truly child?"

Keira nodded silently, not trusting herself to speak.

"I've seen it for myself, sir. She's a gifted Natural." Master Elers confirmed.

"She's a little old to begin training." A thoughtful crinkle appeared in the chancellor's forehead. He turned back to Keira. "Why have you delayed?"

"I know I'm too old, sir. My papa wanted me to be able to marry. And I was frightened of my magic...but...I can't fight it anymore. I don't know how else to explain." She felt her eyes make the shift to silver and clamped her hands over them.

He startled, and Keira flushed with shame. She shoved her power down as far as she could, returning her eyes to their normal green.

The old man blinked at her. "It's been a while since I've seen someone's silver."

"I didn't mean to show it. It happens with strong emotion sometimes, especially if I skip my morning routine."

He waved a hand. "Oh I know all about that. My position demands that I be well informed."

Keira smoothed her skirt again, waiting for something more. She felt Master Elers watching her and glanced up. He had the oddest look on his face, but Keira didn't know him well enough to guess what he might be thinking.

"How do you feel about your king, my dear?" The chancellor asked in his papery voice.

"King Herbert? I love him! Well....I don't know much about him really, but I love his library." She grinned. "What castle resident could complain with such a treasure trove at their fingertips?"

Master Elers snorted softly.

The chancellor gave a reedy chuckle. "I like that attitude, my dear. We will allow you to train, but I must warn you to use caution." He gave her another penetrating look. "A Natural holds a large reserve of power within themselves."

"I give you my word. Thank you." Keira felt light as a feather.

"But will you allow me to train her?" Master Elers asked.

The older man gave a deep sigh. "That is a more complicated matter. I am more well-versed in magic than most, but I cannot claim the expertise of a practicing ArKen. A Natural, at her age... do you believe yourself capable?"

"Yes." He said simply. His shoulders straightened with bravado or confidence. Keira couldn't be sure which.

"Declan, you're a valued agent of His Majesty. I can't approve of you taking risks."

"I don't believe there is any undue risk," Elers asserted. "From what I understand, Miss Smith has her powers reasonably well under control. She would have to, wouldn't she? Or there would have been incidents."

The chancellor opened and closed a book. "Miss Smith, have you ever accidentally used your magic?"

"I...don't think so. I've only used it twice, but I was trying both times." She grimaced. "Neither went well."

The chancellor waved his hand. "That's what teachers are for."

"How badly did the other attempt go?" Elers asked.

"Nobody was hurt. I singed my quilt though. And I always loved that blanket." She set a hand on her stomach, watching the two of them exchange a long look. *Shut up me. Why would they care about my grandmother's quilt?*

"I'll allow this." The king's chancellor turned to her master. "When will you begin?"

"As soon as we can. My apprentice suite is unoccupied, so she should be able to move in immediately."

Apprentice suite? Keira's eyes snapped to him.

"Good. It's best that a budding Natural have her teacher close at hand. Now off you pop." he shooed them from the cluttered office. "My schedule is a bit tight today, but I squeezed you in because it seemed urgent."

Keira curtsied, hands clenched tightly in front of her. "Thank you, Chancellor." She bounced a little on the way up.

Master Elers gave a deeper bow than his first. "I appreciate this chance, Chancellor Nolan."

Keira was a little surprised by how giddy she felt. She was tempted to skip down the hall to tell Arielle. She desperately wanted to tell her oldest friend, Brigid, but that seemed like an in-person sort of announcement. She didn't think she could bring herself to write it in a letter.

"You're welcome. Now, remember — if you need anything, anything at all, do let me know. This is going to change your life more than you may realize. Oh!" He handed her a scroll.

"What's this?"

"An application for the Royal ArKen Apprenticeship Program. If you'd like to work for the crown once you're trained up, the king does provide a small income during training. You would be obligated to seven years of service though. Read it carefully before you decide."

"Thank you." she bobbed another little curtsy before exiting the office.

The door clicked closed behind them and Keira squealed, squirming as she tried to reign in her feelings. She blushed, remembering that she wasn't alone.

"That went well." Master Elers said, grinning as he covered another yawn. "We can get started on your training as soon as you're moved in. Let me know if you need any help."

"I'm really moving in?" Keira asked in a small voice. The application in her hand had driven it from her mind.

He tilted his head. "Of course. It's normal for apprentices. Didn't you live with the midwife who was training you?"

"No."

Elers sighed. "I took the king's coin, and part of that is living quarters with separate rooms for any potential apprentice. Your living quarters are actually across the hall from my own."

"Oh." A weight seemed to lift from her chest. "Yes, that makes sense."

"Follow me."

Keira obeyed, swallowing several questions and instead listening as their footsteps echoed down wide corridors. The castle had never seemed so large, but they soon reached the hallway that held his office, then proceeded around another corner to a hallway that ended abruptly.

"This is my apartment." Elers put his hand on a door, then drew out a key and crossed the wide hall. "And you'll live here."

As she stepped inside, her first thought was that her new rooms were fit for a noble's daughter. Looking around the first room, Keira realized it was actually built for nobility. It was a sitting room, complete with a gargantuan fireplace. The grate must have been twice as large as the one she shared with her parents, and the screen was an ornate thing of whorled iron. Her fingers traced the smooth pattern before she moved on. The hearth was spotless, as was the wide mantlepiece.

The furnishings looked softer than any Keira had seen. The couch and three armchairs were various shades of brown and beige, a good thing given the bold Southern Isles rug that dominated the room. Flowers danced with swirled lines across her floor. Thankfully, it wasn't as bold as Arielle's. Keira's new rug played with muted shades of pink, blue, and brown.

"Are you sure that all of this is mine?"

"You *are* my apprentice."

Elers led her through the wide, rounded arch at the other end of the room. To her surprise, Keira found a corridor. To her left, she opened a wooden door and discovered a small kitchen, complete with its own more modest fireplace and an array of pots and pans. Leaving the door open, Keira moved along, opening each door she came to.

Next was her bedroom. She shuddered at the dimensions, and even more at the size of the bed. It was at least twice as large as what she had. The coverlet was a thing of beauty. There were birds and vines embroidered across it. The background colors were deep green and buttercup yellow. The bed even had what looked like at least a dozen pillows in varying shades of green, yellow, and beige. Deep beige curtains hung around one side of the bed. Keira hadn't known a piece of furniture could be so luxurious. The room also boasted a dresser, wardrobe, and vanity — all in matching mahogany carved with vines. Thick green curtains hung open at the window.

Velvet? Keira wondered in horror. *This room can't be for me.*

Uncomfortable, Keira closed the door and moved on. Elers opened the door across the hall and Keira explored her very own office, complete with a second door that opened on her living room. As she stepped onto the plush floral rug, the improbability of having her own office made tears spring to her eyes. The impossibly large desk looked like it might be oak or some other bright hardwood. A high-backed, cushioned chair stood behind the desk and empty bookshelves of matching wood lined two walls. *Could one person ever have so many books?* Keira shook her head. The chancellor had, as well as Selene and her new Master, but Keira couldn't imagine ever owning so many herself.

Keira stepped back and crossed the hall to find a small bedroom next to the large. It reminded her of her friend Dymphna's room, but a little smaller and with simpler decorations. *Servant's quarters! Am I expected to keep a servant? Will I have to dress in the kinds of clothes that require that much maintenance?* She shook her head. This bedroom seemed like a closer fit for herself than the main room.

The last remaining room was a large bathing room. Keira was shocked to find running water. There was even a place to build a small fire underneath her massive tub. It would be easy to take a hot bath. So much luxury left her speechless and with a strong need to sit down. She did and found a fuzzy seat on her own carved toilet, then stood abruptly, remembering that she was not alone.

Elers led the way back to the corridor outside of her suite. "How long do you expect it to take to move your things?"

Thinking of her own comparatively shabby belongings, Keira flushed. "An hour or two."

"Do you need help moving in? I have to see a few patients, but I can be free this afternoon."

"Oh...no. Thank you, Master." She swept a curtsy she could be proud of. *I'm finally getting the hang of them.*

"That's finally a true title." He grinned. "I won't correct you today. Well, if you can really move in a single day, we'll start your apprenticeship in the morning."

※ ※ ※

The next morning, Keira knocked on her new Master's door. She fought to keep her hand from shaking, but there was nothing she could do about her racing heart. She thought she would feel better if she had been able to talk things through with her parents, but her mother was visiting a friend in the city and her father was busier than ever with work.

Time to stand on my own...apparently.

"Welcome, Apprentice Smith." Her new master greeted her with a deep nod, the ghost of a smile touching his lips.

"Thank you, Master Elers." She curtsied.

His smile solidified. "Declan will do, especially when it's just us. Come in."

Keira stepped into his apartment, fingers absently tugging at the bottom edge of her leather vest. Glancing around with wide eyes, she tried to take everything in. His apartment seemed to have the same layout as hers, although the living room was larger and the colors were darker. He led her into his personal office.

It was nearly an exact copy of her own, with a couple key differences. It was larger, for one, and the plush rug was a deep red, with no floral pattern. More importantly, the bookshelves were full. Rather than too *much* space, it seemed Declan had found them to be too little. He had brought in an extra bookshelf to stand against a third wall, and filled it to maximum capacity as well.

A thick, tidy stack of paper sat on the desk, along with pen, ink, and everything else one would need for a long session of writing. Keira stepped forward, looking around the dim room. Declan produced a trio of soft globes of light and sent them to float near the ceiling.

Keira shivered as the magic thrummed against her skin.

"I prepared this exam for you." Declan explained, gesturing to the stack of paper. "Take your time and answer as completely as you can."

"I thought we already did an exam?" The monotonous memory flooded her mind, but she resisted the groan that wanted to escape her.

"That was the oral exam. I would like to see how you answer given a little more time to think. Please sit." He pulled the chair out for her."

Keira obeyed.

"It's important that you don't look up the answers." He gestured to one of the book shelves. This exam will help me decide where to start your training; you would only be hurting yourself."

"I wouldn't touch your books without permission." Keira murmured to the desktop.

"I'll leave you to it then. There's a water closet at the end of the hall if you need it. I'll join you for lunch. If you finish before then, you can find me in my clinic."

Keira flipped through the sheaf before her. It seemed endless. She looked up at the lights. They had an orange cast, like firelight, but without the flicker. It was softer than the light in the library, but no less useful.

Keira pulled the first page toward herself. The first piece of instructions was to write the alphabet in upper and lower case.

Keira sighed but did her best, embarrassed by her wobbly letters. They were legible, but she didn't write that often, so of course they looked nothing like the example stamped on the page.

The first few pages that followed seemed to have nothing to do with her knowledge. It was a series of puzzles with cryptic instructions. Keira struggled through, enjoying the challenge despite her nerves. As she progressed through the exam, she started to see that some of the puzzles required background knowledge. They grew progressively harder as they transitioned into knowledge-based questions.

Hours passed and her hand seemed permanently cramped. Eventually, Keira went to relieve herself just to stretch her legs. By the time she reached the last page, her stomach was complaining that lunch was late and she had developed a slight headache. The last question was simply to describe her previous education.

Keira had been educated the same way every country peasant was. Her parents taught her to read and do basic arithmetic, as well as the various skills necessary for everyday life. *Does gardening count?* Keira added it. She had already told him that she started training as a midwife in the village, but her family moved before she finished. However, it was her only formal education, so she added that too.

Finished, Keira stood and stretched. The steady light of Master Declan's globes was starting to fade. She stepped through the door into his sitting room and found it empty. The sun slanted through the windows and Keira stepped up to look out. *Mid-afternoon? Have I missed lunch?*

Keira returned and cleaned the pen, then scooped up her sheaf of papers. She found her master in his 'clinic', as he had called it, healing a man with a deep cut on his forearm.

"Are you finished already?"

"Yes, Master. I thought you were joining me for lunch?"

He glanced out the window. "Goodness! I lost track of time."

"Can I help?"

He looked to the patient and the man nodded. Her master held out a hand and she took it.

"Observe. Like you did when I healed you." Declan placed their hands close to the patient's arm.

Keira followed him with her mind, letting a piece of her power flow through his. It was easier than she expected, because all she had to do was sit there, and he could direct it. Layers of the pancakes she had seen before seemed to multiply and join. She blinked in surprise as she saw the skin knit together with her eyes as well as her magic. *Amazing.*

"That's all?" The patient asked. "I didn't realize it was so... thank you, Master Elers."

"I'm glad I could help. Do be more careful." Declan stretched as the patient left.

"That was incredible, Master!"

Declan shrugged. "You did most of the work."

"Did I?"

"Let's get something to eat. I'll take a look at your exam after, but you've done enough for your first day."

* * *

If Keira thought learning magic would be exciting, she was sorely mistaken. The next day, instead of showing her more magic, Declan arrived with a list of books for her to read. He knocked on her door before she was even awake, and Keira slipped into the first dress she touched as quickly as she could manage.

"I'm coming!" She called, stumbling as she tried to squeeze into her boots and walk at the same time.

When Keira opened the door, her master wordlessly handed her a slip of paper. He yawned as she read it, reaching down to adjust a baggy sleeve. It contained a long list of books, sorted by category and numbered in a confusing fashion. Each category seemed to have been given a letter, and numbers between one and four were placed in front of them. But there were two books labeled '1A' and none for '2B' or '4C'.

"What's this?"

"Your curriculum. We'll be covering the topics labeled with a one first."

Keira looked down at the list. There were eight books labeled one. Judging from their titles, none of them was about medicine or magic.

"You look like you have a question."

"No magic?" Keira was surprised to find disappointment threading its way through her relief.

He shook his head, "Magic isn't your problem. You have plenty of power, which means you'll need to study harder than anyone."

"That doesn't make sense."

"Most new ArKen make a lot of mistakes with very little consequence, but as a Natural you're capable of doing a lot more damage than a Seeker. Instead of risking only your own life, you risk everyone near you. I expect a future healer to take that risk seriously."

Keira agreed, then asked her other burning question. "No medicine?"

He laughed, "That's higher level learning. You'll need a solid foundation for context."

Keira frowned, unconvinced.

"I can assure you, I've built this curriculum with your interest in healing in mind."

Scanning the list again, Keira felt a little dizzy at the idea of such expense. "Does the library have these?"

"They should have most of the texts you'll need for our first unit of study."

Keira's shoulders relaxed and then tensed again. He had said first unit. As much as she hated the idea of owing the king seven years of her life, the sheer number of texts Declan had listed boggled her mind. Thinking of the library, her mind drifted back to the orbs that floated near the ceiling and the way they had drawn her in.

"Can people sense magic?"

"What do you mean?"

"Like the lights you use for your office. Or when you heal someone?"

"There's nothing to sense unless your magic is crossing another's."

Keira frowned. "That doesn't make any sense. Magic exists, so it must be there to sense."

He sighed. "You have me there, but your senses won't extend beyond yourself and your work. There's no way to sense magic unless it intersects your own power."

Unwilling to contradict him again, Keira swallowed her next question and returned to her list. It looked like years of study, but she couldn't be sure. "How long will I spend on each unit?"

"There's no standard answer. I selected these based on your current level of education and we'll move as quickly as you learn." He smiled. "I was impressed by how well you did in life sciences and medicine, even with your unfinished apprenticeship."

"Thank you. So I just read these?"

"No. I expect you to study them. You should know them as well as you know yourself. We'll spend time reviewing your reading together, but I have office hours to maintain, so learn what you can in your downtime as well."

"How long are your hours?" Keira asked.

"It's less the length and more that they're limited. I took the king's coin when I was still training so my work is a little less independently directed than many ArKen. I have a soft cap at fifty hours and I'm forbidden from working more than sixty....Nolan can be a real pain" He made a face of exaggerated horror. "I have a time sheet and there are *consequences* if I go over. Like forced vacation days."

Keira giggled. "You must enjoy your work. But if you work for the king, does he ever ask you to do things other than healing?"

Declan's eyebrows knit together and Keira thought she had said something to upset him. But when he answered, it was with a thoughtful tone. "You've hit on the reason my father wanted me to refuse the offer. The king has every right to redirect my work. He hasn't, but I'm most suited to healing. Most ArKen find they excel in one or two areas over others. As a Natural, you'll likely have wider specialization than typical, but healers are in high demand. Requesting the position is little more than a formality."

"But it can happen? I've been thinking about it, but I'm afraid I'd be asked to hurt people. What made you decide to apply? I thought you were already a noble?" Keira bit her lip, afraid her question was too personal.

His delayed response seemed to confirm her doubt, but he didn't seem offended. Rather, the faintest pink at the tips of his ears made her think he might be embarrassed. "I'm a third son. My elder brother had promised me a home, but I will never inherit any land myself. Rather than live as a burden, reading my books in some forgotten corner of my brother's property, I figured I ought to do something useful with my time." He shrugged. "There was more to it than that, but it's the best explanation I can give."

Seven

Keira tossed and turned, the heavy covers making her feel trapped. A dream clung to the edges of her consciousness, but she was too stressed to fall back asleep. The application for becoming a 'King's Apprentice', as the form called it, still lay on her end table. It had been a full week since their meeting, but she was no closer to making her decision. She glared at it, but the rolled parchment just sat there innocently.

Giving up, Keira sighed. She rolled out of bed and dressed quickly. She briefly considered a morning ride, but their mule didn't like mornings and the sky looked a little dark. Keira paused to stretch, still wondering what to do with herself.

Library. Glancing back at the end table, Keira returned to snatch the application. Selene was a morning person. If she had some free time, maybe Keira could ask her about taking the king's coin.

It seemed only moments later that Keira knocked softly on Selene's office door.

Selene opened the door with a hand buried in her half-squashed curls, yawning widely. Her clothes were rumpled in a way that made Keira think she had fallen asleep at her desk.

"Are you planning to make a habit of these visits?" Selene asked.

Keira grimaced. Had she woken her? "I hope you don't mind the company."

She smiled. "No, but I have to start work soon."

"Oh." Keira said, shuffling backward. "I can stop in another time."

"Soon isn't now." Selene eyed her. "What's on your mind?"

Keira traced a shape in the carpet with her toes. "I've gotten permission from the king's chancellor to pursue my gift...and I'm in need of some advice on my apprenticeship."

"I thought we talked about that. My work is very specialized. I hope you aren't thinking of me as a potential Master. I wouldn't be an adequate teacher for a Natural." True to her habit, Selene spoke twice the words someone else might have, in half the time. She waved Keira into the room and filled two cups with water.

"No." Keira said when Selene took a breath.

"I don't know any of the other ArKen. I spend most of my time in my office. I'm sorry, but we don't have a guild or anything — it's a highly individual profession. Well, I know their names and faces, and I greet them in the corridors, but I certainly don't know any well enough to recommend them as a tutor." She shrugged.

"Oh, that's not the advice I needed. I already *have* an apprenticeship."

"That's wonderful!" Selene passed her a cup of floral tea and waved her into a chair.

Rain pattered against the windows, the cold making the glass fog up.

"May I ask a personal question?" Keira said.

"Certainly."

"Did you take the king's coin during your training?" Keira handed the contract to her.

Selene took a few moments to read it before answering, "This program didn't exist when I was learning. That was a good twenty years ago now."

Keira frowned. "You don't look old enough to have been a Mistress for twenty years."

Selene laughed hard enough her words sounded strangled. "Flattery will get you everywhere."

"I wasn't-"

"It is something to consider carefully. Seven years is a long time."

Keira wrapped both hands around her steaming teacup before asking her next question, "How did you get your position?"

Selene shrugged. "I interviewed with Arielle's parents. Then the chancellor approved my appointment. They mostly use me as a shadow scribe, though occasionally the knights will ask for weather predictions."

"Oh...when Arielle said you were a weather mage I assumed it was stuff like calling lightning and making it snow."

Selene gave a hearty laugh, "I can make it sprinkle a little if there's already a lot of humidity. But I'm not powerful enough for what you're talking about. Few are."

"What's a shadow scribe?"

"When I write out a copy of a book, I can make more copies — as long as I have paper and ink laid out."

"Really?"

"I can do four shadow copies at once." She grinned. "I've never heard of another shadow scribe who could manage that many. It takes a precise focus."

The conversation meandered through smaller matters as the two finished their tea. Keira could feel the unseasonable cold leach through the windows, but instead of making her shiver it added to the cozy atmosphere. She suspected it would storm later, but she sat surrounded by books with a hot cup of tea in her hands. *And good company,* Keira decided. Selene was a pleasant companion, neither too eager to fill silence nor difficult to talk to.

"How did you like my book?" Selene asked after a while.

"It was fascinating! The chapter on dew and frost especially. I was struck by the way you described..." Keira continued gushing about her favorite parts for a few minutes.

Selene laughed. "I think you must be the only person who's read it so attentively. I *am* glad you enjoyed it, but I do have to get started on work." She pulled a stack of paper towards herself and reached for ink and pen.

"Thank you for speaking with me, Selene. I appreciate your time." Keira bobbed a shallow curtsy.

"Any time. And I do mean that. Visit again." Selene smiled and waved her off.

Keira wandered for a while, still thinking about the choice that lay ahead. The sun rose fully outside and she decided it was finally late enough to go for a ride. It would be nice to clear her head. Rain had started tapping at the windows so archery was out of the question, but she knew Cinnamon wouldn't mind getting a bit wet.

* * *

Keira's eyes snapped open. The gray half-light of predawn made her coverlet look washed out. Her fingers traced one of the bright birds stitched into her blanket. *How long do I have to wait?*

Today was the day that Master Declan had said they would meet to discuss her progress. She wiggled out of bed and into her second nicest dress, soft muslin in a bright cornflower blue. Keira squirmed with nerves, but managed to get her feet into their boots and her hair into a braid over her shoulder.

As soon as she was dressed, she set about collecting the books she had been studying. They seemed to have scattered themselves throughout the week. She found three in her office, two in the living room, and one hiding under her bed. As she strained to reach, the tricksy thing skidded away from her. Keira had to fetch another book to push it out the other side of the bed. *I'm lucky the bed doesn't sit against the wall,* she mused as she caught her breath.

After a cup of tea and an apple from her very own fruit bowl, Keira tugged her clothing into tidiness and slipped into the hall. She didn't realize she had forgotten her heavy stack of books until after she knocked. It took a long time for Declan to come to the door. First, she worried that he hadn't heard her, then that it was too early. But when he opened the door, it was with a friendly smile — or at least what passed for one from him; the corners of his lips were slightly turned up and his eyes were bright.

"Ready to get started?"

She bit her lip and nodded.

Declan led her to his study. The plush red carpet silenced their footfalls as he gestured her to a chair. He sat behind the desk and folded his hands in front of himself. Then he leaned forward to ask the first question of the morning.

"How far did you get?"

Keira did her best to describe where she had stopped in each book. Elers raised his eyebrows, but made no comment. It made her nervous. *Have I done well or did my slow reading hold me back?* Keira buried her booted toes into the carpet.

That question was followed by dozens more. Her nerves faded as the questions continued. They got progressively more difficult, but Keira didn't begin to struggle until the second hour. Around that time, Master Eler's servant brought them a pot of tea and some fluffy bread. Keira ate it in small bites, marveling at the soft texture. At long last, after they had begun a third hour of questioning, Declan leaned back and crossed his arms.

"How am I doing, Master?" She asked, mouth dry. She took a sip of her cold tea.

"I believe we can move on to the next stage of your training."

"Shadowing you in the clinic?" Keira suggested hopefully.

"Soon, but first we have to get you comfortable controlling your abilities."

"How do we do that?" She asked, glancing down at her hands as her heart fluttered in her chest.

"Cautiously."

Declan rose and walked to a cabinet, where he withdrew three rocks. "First, we'll work on your extrasensory perception. Expanding it will help you to understand and control your powers outside of your own body."

"So what are the rocks for?"

"I want you to tell me which one contains a fossil."

Keira closed her eyes for the briefest of moments. Because she had skipped her morning archery, her magic already reached grasping tendrils out. "They all do."

"You're mistaken."

Keira bit her lip, but shook her head. "The fossils in the limestone are tiny, but there's no mistaking the trace of life."

"The 'trace of life'?" He asked, eyebrows sliding together.

"Yes. You can't feel it?"

He shook his head, frowning. His eyes had a faraway look, like she might lose him to some line of thought, then he nodded and returned his attention to her. "For the purposes of this exercise, which rock contains a fossil that would be visible to the human eye?"

"The middle one. It contains some sort of bony fish."

"Correct. I'm impressed that you could tell the type of fossil. And….if what you say about the limestone is accurate than you may have a future relying on this sense."

"I don't want to be a natural historian."

"This is the same sense that helped me rebuild the web of nerves in your skin. A delicate extrasensory perception will be instrumental in your work as a healer."

"Oh." Keira fell silent.

Clearly, this was a skill she wanted. She rather suspected it was already hers though. Keira closed her eyes and listened. She could feel every creature within five hundred feet. She absently wondered how far this sense could reach, if she tried.

Declan tapped her shoulder. "Stay with me, Kei."

"How far can an ArKen extend this sense?" She asked, blinking in surprise at the diminutive.

"I believe the average is somewhere around two hundred feet." He said after a moment's consideration. "I can reach a little further, but not much."

Keira clamped her mouth shut on her next question. How could she explain, when she didn't understand it herself? *How far can I reach if I try?*

"I think we should run some experiments and see how far you can push your awareness." Declan said, echoing her private wishes.

"Alright. How should we do that?" She asked, grinning.

"Close your eyes, take some deep breaths, and focus." He instructed.

She fought a giggle. That was the advice in all the books, but never seemed necessary. She obeyed nonetheless. Keira stretched her awareness to see how far she could push it, and was surprised when she felt the kitchen workers running around three floors below them, and birds in the air above the castle. After a few minutes, she realized she could feel her father working in the forge. Another deep breath and she found a familiar raven sitting on top of the shed by the archery range.

"Impossible." She whispered as she found a stablehand brushing Cinnamon.

She smiled. The mule was thoroughly enjoying the attention and nosing in the man's pocket for a cube of sugar.

Cinnamon snorted a greeting to her.

Hello to you too.

"Can we talk with our minds?" Keira asked without opening her eyes.

"In an emergency, possibly, but it would not be clear enough for everyday speech."

"May I try it?" She persisted.

"Sure."

Hello Declan. She sent gently, *I can hear my family's mule being groomed.*

"Impossible," he mouthed.

"Could you hear me?"

"I could." He shook his head, "Words too, not just an impression. Can you really hear that, all the way from the castle?"

"Yes. He's enjoying himself, but he seemed happy I visited."

"Wait....you meant you could hear his....thoughts?"

"Is that unusual? Aside from the distance, I mean."

He folded his arms and took a moment to answer. "Sending to an animal isn't entirely unheard of."

"How rare is it?"

"I'd say one in twenty ArKen can do it. Probably a higher percentage of Naturals."

Keira took a minute to process that. "So....does this mean we're done working on my...extrasensory perception? Is that the right term?"

He shook his head. "We're far from done. It can always be improved, even if yours is already impressive. It does mean that we can move on to the next stage of training, however. Kinesis."

"What's that?" She straightened in her seat.

"Moving things without touching them. It's one of the safest things for a new ArKen to experiment with, and will help you gain fine control of your magic." He grimaced. "We'll start with something soft. I have to warn you to expect the unexpected. I started with a scarf and it took a while before I could do anything with it. My first attempt, it didn't move, and several attempts after that. The first time it did move, I threw it at the wall. And my second time, I set it on fire. Seventeenth time was the charm."

"I'm eager to try."

He reached into a drawer and pulled out a clean linen bandage. "Play with this then. It won't hurt if you throw it. I'm going to check if I have any patients."

Keira accepted the linen, running it through her fingers to get a feel for it. She could feel her eyes shift to gray and then silver as she manipulated the cloth. It was easier than she expected. She amused herself for a good fifteen minutes while Declan was gone, but a bandage could only be bent in so many ways. She briefly wondered why there weren't performances like this, but it got old faster than she expected.

At the peak of her boredom, Keira stood up and wielded the linen bandage like a sword, performing a clumsy facsimile of a pattern dance she had seen some of the castle guards do. It was pretty fun, until Declan entered the room with Fionn Duval. Keira colored as if she had been caught doing something shameful.

"I didn't know you danced." Fionn teased with a crooked smile.

"I don't. Maybe at parties."

"I'll hold you to that." Fionn said with a crooked smile.

Is he flirting? But Keira didn't have time to process her own question because Declan cut into her thoughts.

"That was amazing!" He exclaimed, "How long did it take until you could manipulate it like that?"

Keira could feel her eyes returning to their normal frog green as she wrapped the linen back up. "It didn't take any time. I've just been twisting it around while you were gone."

"No time?"

Keira shrugged. "It's not very heavy. I should probably try this with something else."

"Maybe you should just move on to the next thing?' Fionn glanced at Declan.

Keira shook her head. "Magic is dangerous. I don't want to move on until I'm ready."

"You're ready." Declan said with a tone of finality.

"If you're sure." Keira hugged herself. She didn't feel the same certainty. "What's next?"

"We'll try the same thing, but with projectiles."

Keira gave him a quizzical look.

"You are an archer?" Her master looked to Fionn for confirmation and received a nod.

"How will that help me heal people?" Keira asked tentatively.

"You'd be surprised. You want fine kinetic control if you'll be using your magic to heal."

"Makes sense to me." Fionn agreed with a shrug.

"Very well." Keira sighed. "Will you accompany me to the practice range?"

"Yes." Declan nodded.

"So how are we doing this, Master Declan?" Keira asked as she strung her bow.

It was a beautiful day, probably one of the last real days of summer weather. The air was hot, but dry. Keira enjoyed the warmth of the sun on her shoulders and in her hair. A breeze blew as she settled herself into the state of awareness that meant she was interacting with her magic. It felt like the cool underside of a leaf. *Or the good side of a pillow.* She took a slow breath, trying to maintain the feeling. For most of her life, she had believed she could never feel this relaxed with her power; it was good to know that she had been wrong.

Declan pointed. "Shoot in that direction."

"What? That would be dangerous. There's no target."

"That's the point." Fionn laughed. "He wants you to hit the target."

"I can try, but can we at least set a target in that direction? I don't want my arrow to fly off and hit someone."

Fionn walked to the next target and tried to lift it. "This is heavier than it looks. A little help Declan?"

They tried to lift it, but gave up after a few minutes of struggling.

"How about facing the equipment shed?" Declan asked.

Keira faced it, but wasn't comfortable firing until Fionn checked that it was empty.

"Are you sure I can do this?" Keira asked, "What if it flies wildly? Arrows move so fast!"

"I can protect us." Declan replied. "It's perfectly safe. Nobody's coming, right?"

Keira extended her senses, then shook her head.

"Do your worst." Declan said with a rare grin, "The timid dragon has the smallest hoard."

"And lives the longest." She muttered to herself as she lined up her shot. Keira took a deep breath to steady herself, then fired. Her first arrow struck the shed in front of her with an awful sound and she flinched. She had barely managed to keep her magical perception on it as it moved.

Keira took a deep breath and fired again. Her second arrow struck the grass to her right. *Closer.* She followed up with another shot before she could forget how she had done that. It did not strike the shed in front of her, but it also didn't hit the target she aimed for. It embedded itself in the edge of the target next to it.

Her fourth arrow struck the shed, but the next three found their home near the center of the target she aimed for. It seemed to be a matter of "seeing" with her magic instead of her eyes.

"Excellent!" Declan yelled after the last arrow struck.

"You're amazing!" Fionn laid an arm across her shoulders and shook her. "Way to go."

"I think I might have been doing this more subtly for a long time, without noticing." Keira confessed. "Ever since I gained awareness of the magical energy in my body it's gotten much easier to hit the target."

Declan considered. "Show me how you normally shoot."

Keira turned to face her target, breathing in her environment, and let loose half a dozen arrows. It was just the same as it had been every morning since she discovered her own personal form of meditation. Her awareness of her form flowed through her as her body moved. This time, she could feel Declan follow her with his mind. She tried to ignore him as she moved, but it was a little distracting. Her last arrow flew wide.

By the time she finished he was laughing.

"What?" She demanded hotly.

"You aren't doing anything. If it's easier it's just because you're more in tune with your body."

Keira breathed a sigh of relief. "Good."

The raven that liked to sit on the shed swooped down and landed on a nearby fencepost. Fionn yelped, but Keira held up a scrap of meat. Her archery companion snapped it up, then flew off.

"He likes to join me in the mornings." She laughed, enjoying their surprise.

"I've never seen a raven act like that."

Keira shrugged, "He knows I won't hurt him, and I usually have something good to eat."

"How does he know you won't hurt him?" Fionn asked.

"Because...I never have."

"Keira can talk to animals." Declan explained.

She huffed. "I didn't know that until today. He does seem to like me though."

"I'm sure feeding him has nothing to do with it." Fionn said dryly. He clapped his hands together and rubbed them. "So what's next?"

"More practice?" Keira guessed.

The three of them stayed at the top of the hill for two hours. Keira sank arrow after arrow into her targets, then called them back to her hand using her new kinetic abilities. She was satisfied that she had control after the first hour, but Declan had her keep going.

The second half of her practice was a lot more interesting than the first. It came as a shock the first time Declan fought against her and she missed. She was ready for him the next time though. Her arrow sank deeply into her target, but snapped in half with the force of her magic. Before long, Keira was sending three arrows at a time, and fighting against Declan's will. Then she tried four. Four, it seemed, was too many. Declan redirected two of them consistently.

Finally, he raised a hand in the hair. "Time to stop. I'm exhausted."

Keira froze in shock when she turned around to face her teacher. He looked like he'd been awake for three days. Dark circles had appeared under his eyes and his shoulders drooped.

"Are you ok?" She asked softly, guilt erasing her smile.

"I'll be fine." Declan grimaced, shivering. "I was hoping I could beat you. This is a good lesson in what happens when magic is overused. Pay attention."

She nodded seriously. Now that she wasn't focused on her arrows, Keira could feel that the magic beyond his personal barrier was greatly depleted.

"Are you sure you're alright?" Keira asked. "Can I add some of my strength to yours?"

He shook his head, "It doesn't work like that, but all I need is a bit of rest."

Fionn squeezed Declan's shoulder and looked down at Keira. "Relax. I'll stay with him until he feels better."

"Take the rest of the afternoon off, Kei. Do something fun." Declan yawned.

Keira curtsied as she would have to a noble before she started her training, "Yes, Master."

She watched Fionn help Declan back to the castle. He didn't seem to need much help, but Fionn hovered over his friend like a worried mother hen. Keira sat down and soaked in the sunshine for a bit, then headed for the stables. No doubt Cinnamon would like a ride. It would be nice to spend some time doing something other than working on her magic.

Eight

Keira spent the ensuing fortnight shadowing Declan in the clinic. It felt like her training as a healer had finally, truly begun. While she wasn't allowed to touch the patients, Keira followed with her senses and added her strength to her master's. It didn't take long for her to realize that Declan needed that strength those first few days. Apparently, overusing magic was more costly than she realized.

At the end of her time in the clinic, Declan gave her a new list of books to study. Unfortunately, after spending most of the following morning hunting through the shelves of the castle library with Arielle, Keira was forced to admit that roughly half of them would need to be purchased. At least she had more than a month to get them. Declan had told her to prepare for their first unit exam at the end of the second month of autumn.

Keira collapsed onto one of the blazing-orange stools in the staff room with a sigh.

"I'm sorry I couldn't be more help." Arielle's soft voice carried across the room as she bustled around the larder for their lunch.

"You helped plenty." Keira rubbed her temples, her mind still on the coin. Her parents might be able to afford a volume or two, but seven? Not a chance.

Arielle took another stool at the tiny table, tossed her long braid over her shoulder, and set a full plate of sandwiches between them. "Did you ever make up your mind about taking the king's coin?"

Keira still hadn't made a final decision. Four years of training, plus seven in service would be a great portion of her life. From what she'd read, ArKen did tend to live a little longer, although she suspected that had less to do with magic than general knowledge of medicine. Either way, it wouldn't make a decade pass any faster. She was befuddled. For once, her father had not given a final decision. He opposed it, but he hadn't forbidden it.

"I keep thinking I've decided to do it and then the next hour I think I couldn't possibly."

"Why?" Arielle asked as she took a dainty bite.

The utter lack of guile in her wide brown eyes loosened something in Keira's chest.

"I'm afraid." She admitted, wrapping one arm around her stomach. Despite the fire crackling merrily at her back, cold crept up her spine and into her scalp. Her eyes stung as she dropped her food and turned to her friend. "I don't know what's wrong with me. I just keep thinking 'what if'. If I say yes, the king owns me for seven years. What if he asks me to serve in the guard? And if Ravena goes to war during that time. The last thing in the world that I want to be is a battlemage."

"Healers are rare." Arielle squeezed her hand. "Do you really think that's likely?"

"No..."

Her friend tilted her head and stared at her for a long moment before asking her next question. "What else is holding you back?"

Keira could only nod. She hadn't let herself think about it, but there was one more thing. "I told my parents when I started training that I knew I was giving up on marrying. It just isn't in the cards for me."

Arielle gave a very unladylike snort. Keira almost couldn't

believe it had come from her quiet friend. She stared, shocked enough that the tears that had threatened her dried up.

"Your thinking is flawed."

"In other words, I'm a troll-head?"

"I didn't say that!"

"Well, *you* wouldn't." Keira teased with a weak smile.

Arielle sighed. "Well, you aren't a troll-head, but you're still thinking about this all wrong. ArKen marry all the time."

"Sure, Seekers from the nobility marry other nobles. Naturals almost never marry, and I don't have the advantage of noble blood."

Arielle actually rolled her eyes. "*Keira*, think about this for a minute. Noble houses are absolutely plagued with politics. Of course Naturals don't marry nobles. Well, at least not often. When they do, historically it has been someone from an exceptionally high rank, or someone unlanded. And plenty of Naturals have married among the gentry or peasantry." She took an overlarge bite of her sandwich.

Keira sighed. "I always expected to marry. And I don't think there's anything I want more than to become a mother. I just...I couldn't keep denying this power singing through my blood. I would have if it were possible."

"I think you're giving up too soon. If you feel in your bones that you're meant to marry, I think it will happen for you. You just have to find the right guy. Maybe you already have." She smirked.

"What? Who?"

Arielle gave another, softer snort. "You haven't noticed the way Fionn Duval flirts with you?"

"He does not!" Keira's stomach gave a swoop even as she denied it.

Arielle fiddled with the silver locket she wore and blushed. "Well, you wouldn't be the only one with your heart set on a noble son."

"What?" Keira stood, forgetting the remnants of their lunch entirely and almost knocking over the tiny wooden table.

"I don't think he's noticed my feelings, but I do enjoy conversations with Declan Elers." Arielle blushed still deeper. "We've been taking turns annotating books for each other."

"Aww." If there was any way to Declan's heart, Keira suspected that would be it.

* * *

Once again, it only took a few days to arrange a meeting with the king's chancellor. Keira was flattered that he chose to see her personally for their second meeting, rather than sending her to one of his numerous assistants. She brought her application for the program with her, still unsigned. She needed to ask her questions first. They had their meeting early in the morning, about three weeks into her apprenticeship with Declan.

She was relieved by her lack of nerves this time. She was unconcerned about her appearance. She had taken extra care with her braid that morning, but was wearing her simple brown dress and the boots she wore daily. The chancellor was one of the least intimidating people she had ever met. His position could have made him nigh unapproachable, but he reminded her of one of the grandfathers back in Stoneybrooke.

When she was called in, she found his office just as cluttered as it had been the first time. Bookshelves and barrels full of scrolls lined the edges of the room. If anything, they were more overstuffed than last time, although the desk itself was a bit neater. The chancellor smiled warmly as she curtsied. He gestured for her to sit, the maroon fabric of his robe sliding across his desk. Luckily, he was occupied with a cup of tea this morning instead of a pot of ink. It smelled wonderfully fruity.

"Miss Smith, I'm glad to see you again. I understand you've made quite the impression on your Master."

"I don't know what you mean, sir."

He peered at her through his small glasses. "He seems to think you'll be quite the ArKen by the time your training is complete. Are you still happy with your decision, Apprentice Smith?" The chancellor peered up at her as he poured a second cup of tea.

"Yes sir." She smiled. "It isn't as exciting as I thought it would be, but I'm not sure that's a bad thing."

"Excitement is overrated."

"I don't disagree, sir." And she didn't. Between burning her hands and the prospect of attending a party full of nobles in a little over a month, she had quite enough excitement to last for a long while.

"I believe you had questions about the apprenticeship program?" He folded back his maroon sleeve to take a sip of his tea.

Keira picked hers up to banish the autumn chill from her fingertips and give her hands something to do before she answered, "Yes, sir. I did."

"You did?"

"I do."

He blinked at her, waiting for her to continue.

"I'm almost certain that I want to apply." Keira shifted awkwardly and bit her lower lip.

"What is it that's holding you back, my dear?" He leaned forward, "Come now child. There's no need to be shy."

"What exactly is expected of you during your time in the king's service? And do you get to choose your field of magic while you work for him?"

"Nothing unusual. The ArKen that work for His Majesty set their own hours for the most part, as long as they keep working, the king doesn't complain. You turn in a time sheet at the end of each month."

"How many hours is generally expected per week?" Keira asked. She couldn't remember anything Declan had said about the time and difficulty of the position, other than the upper limit.

"Between thirty-five and fifty. You would be paid by the hour, but His Majesty does not permit his ArKen to work more than that. It's demanding work."

Keira laughed. "Master Elers said up to sixty."

"Yes, well....he likes to push the boundaries. He gets away with it because he is our most capable healer. And yes, you do get to pick your field of work."

"Guaranteed? The Crown will never require you to change it if you're capable of wider usefulness?" Keira could feel her eyes misting as she stared intently at the chancellor.

"Miss Smith, I can tell you mean to ask something important, but you're dancing around the subject. What is it that you actually wish to know?"

"My magic is strong." Keira's thumb drew a circle on the warm teacup. "I want to heal people. If I take the king's coin...is there any chance he will ask me to hurt them instead? I don't want to be a battlemage. *Ever.*" Keira felt her eyes moisten with her last statement.

"Ah, I see." The chancellor leaned back in his chair. "Healers are in high demand, but I can't guarantee it. The only way it would ever happen is if we went to war, but we're generally shorter on healers than soldiers. Most ArKen never even try to learn healing. It's quite specialized. And there is no real threat of war. King Herbert has managed to secure an even longer peace than the record his grandfather set."

Keira nodded, signed her form with only a small twinge of anxiety, and slid it across the desk.

"Welcome to the Royal ArKen Apprenticeship Program." The chancellor said with a little seated bow.

* * *

The next morning, Keira stepped hesitantly into the front room of Declan's workspace. The overlarge sitting area looked much the same as the last time she had been there. The stacks of leaflets on the end tables sat in tidy piles, and only a few globe lights floated in the corners, making it clear that Declan hadn't yet opened to patients. Keira bit her lip, but carried on. It was too late in the morning for her master to be in his rooms.

She poked her head through the open door of the inner office and found Declan sitting behind his birchwood desk, completely absorbed in his paperwork. Fionn lounged in one of the armchairs and waved her into the other. Keira sat with a shy smile for Fionn before turning back to Declan. His eyes were glued to the page.

She tossed her intricately braided hair over one shoulder and waited for her master to notice her. Keira was exceedingly proud of herself — she had spent a tedious half hour braiding her hair using the same magic she had learned only a few days before. It had turned out far neater, and yet was more complex, than any braid she had ever done by hand.

Fionn cleared his throat.

Declan looked up and started. "Keira!"

"I hope it's alright that I came to see you; I didn't mean to interrupt."

"Of course, of course." He shuffled the papers, then stopped to rub his eyes.

How long has he been working? Sunrise couldn't have been more than an hour ago. Keira bit her lip.

Declan straightened with a yawn, but brightened as he turned toward her. "How are your studies coming?"

Keira grinned and flipped her braid again. "Look and see."

"Look?" He frowned.

"I used the kineses thing you showed me to braid my hair."

"You did *what*!?" Declan asked in a barely recognizable voice. It was soft, but so tightly controlled she was surprised the words had made it through.

Keira had never seen Declan angry before. He always looked a little distracted, which some people mistook for angry, but he was one of the more even tempered people she knew. That's why it took her by such surprise to see his nostrils go white as he scowled at her. She found herself scooting back in her chair, and couldn't quite make eye contact with him.

"It looks lovely." Fionn offered, breaking the tension.

Keira blushed, but returned the smile he gave her.

"There is a reason I asked you not to practice magic on your own. You could have hurt yourself. More than hurt." Declan shoved the heels of his hands into his eyes. "Don't you remember what happened when you tried a globe light on your own?"

"I'm sorry, Master."

He sighed. "Sorry doesn't reattach scalps."

Keira gulped at the visceral image that flashed through her mind. "It won't happen again. You have my word."

"See that it doesn't."

The silence stretched between them.

"How did your meeting go?" Fionn asked before it could grow too awkward.

"I joined the Royal ArKen Apprenticeship Program."

"I think you made the right choice. I've never regretted mine." Declan looked up at a knock on the door. "Come in."

Keira looked up to see Arielle's willowy frame sidle into the room. She had a book tucked into the crook of her elbow. One dark hand fiddled with her necklace.

"Ari, what brings you here?" A warm smile softened his features for a moment before it dropped away and was replaced by a wrinkle between his eyebrows. "Is your mother well?"

"Oh! Yes. I was just..." Arielle's long fingers jumped from the locket to the edge of the book. "I have another book for you, but you're busy. I didn't realize."

She started to back away, but Fionn jumped to his feet with a mischievous glint in his eyes. "Keira's lessons will last all day. Declan can spare a moment." He dropped an arm across her shoulders and led her to his now-vacant seat.

Arielle plopped into the chair with a smile that looked almost painful. "Thank you."

"You brought me something?" Declan asked after an awkward moment, but Keira could see the light in his eyes.

"The author was an ArKen naturalist and healer. It was an interesting read, even if many of his ideas have been debunked." Arielle slid it across the desk, blushing furiously. "I left some notes behind."

Declan thumbed through the book with what appeared to be genuine interest as Arielle asked Keira about her meeting with the chancellor. Whatever the odd tension was, it seemed to dissipate. Fionn gave a disappointed sigh and Keira couldn't help but agree.

* * *

The following weeks passed in a haze of eye strain. Keira spent most of her time studying — sometimes with Arielle, sometimes with Declan — but her favorite study buddy was Fionn. Somehow, it was easier to keep herself from getting frustrated with difficult subjects when he was around. It was like his natural confidence was contagious....and if she was honest with herself, she just enjoyed his company.

The biggest interruption to her studies was a fire in the marketplace. It resulted in a shortage of some herbs Declan used in his clinic, so Keira, Arielle, Declan, and Fionn spent a long and muddy afternoon combing the nearest wood for the missing remedies only to return dripping and shivering, mostly empty-handed. There were rumors too, unnerving ones. There was talk of bandit raids along the western border — and whether they were really bandits or something more official. A merchant staying in the castle absolutely insisted messages were being carried between King Herbert and the King of Eimar, their nearest neighbor to the east.

Keira did her best to focus on her studies. These weren't the sorts of problems she could do anything about. All she could do was pray that she wasn't training to be a healer for nothing. It felt like the chances of her being called on to do the opposite were only growing. But she had already taken the king's coin and, at this point, there was no going back. She reasoned that the better she became at healing, the more valuable she would be in that position and the less likely to be called on to do anything else.

* * *

"And what would you give to a patient who presented with stomach upset and arm pain?" Declan quizzed.

"Acetylsalicylic acid." Keira responded confidently. "As a precaution, but I would listen to their heart afterward to see if there was a blockage."

"And what would you do if you found one?" He raised an eyebrow.

"Once my training is complete, I would ease it myself."

"Your training is not complete, so what would you do?"

"Call you, Master Declan." She grinned.

He had shown her how to clear a blockage from a vessel on a model, but there was no way to practice that use of her magic on a living creature unless it actually happened. Keira would prefer to go without the practice. It was knowledge she hoped she would never need.

"And what if a farmer were to come in with a scythe embedded in their torso? I've seen that one before."

"I would keep them calm and make sure that the implement remained immobile. Then I would call you."

"What if I did not come?" He asked so fast it sounded like an extension of her answer.

"I would send an animal to find you."

"What if they could not?"

"I'd call for the medic from the guard."

"And if he wouldn't come?"

"I suppose if there were no other choice, I would assess the damage myself and attempt to knit the tissue together as I slowly removed the implement. But I would call another ArKen before it came to that. Anyone who had full control of their abilities would be helpful."

"Good. You're not overeager to test your own gift on a patient."

She shuddered and shook her head, "No. The last thing they need is to be used as a training experiment."

"What would you do for a fever? If you were in full control of your abilities. Say I was no longer your master."

Keira listed several herbal remedies. "Though if it was a low grade fever, I would probably just stick to a cool cloth and hydration."

"Good."

"And for a sprain?"

"Rest, ice, compression, and elevation." She said without hesitation.

Declan had been quizzing her in this manner all afternoon — long enough for her back to start hurting. Her office chair was not quite as comfortable as she had first thought. And the questions had flown so quickly that her answers felt rushed. *How does Declan even remember his next question?* In contrast, Declan looked perfectly comfortable, his posture unusually straight, his face open, wide brown eyes unblinking as always.

But if she passed this lengthy test —and it was a big if — then she would be allowed to shadow him with his patients on a regular basis, lending her strength to his. She would not be permitted to direct any magical healing for a long time yet, but Keira would be trusted to mix simple medicines and clean and bandage minor wounds. It was slow going, but in the last couple of weeks she had started receiving some responsibilities.

"How am I doing, Master?" She asked.

"So far, quite well. I think we will move on to the next stage of your training."

"Shadowing you in the clinic?" Keira asked, voice rising in her excitement.

"Shadowing me in the clinic." He confirmed, a rare grin splitting his usually serious face. "Welcome to clinicals."

* * *

"I'm surprised you hadn't heard." Dymphna snipped a thread and glanced over at Arielle.

"Of *course* the stables are empty." Arielle smoothed the elegant dress in her own lap. She was picking threads loose to free expensive lace from one of Duchess Duval's old dresses. "People don't feel safe on the road right now, with the disappearing shipments. No one wants to travel, even to visit the king."

"It's a bit silly, really. The only caravans that have been attacked were bound for Fort Ravemar. There's no reason anyone else shouldn't feel safe." Dymphna said, her eyes glued to a stubborn stitch.

"That's easy to say when we're sitting comfortably in the capital." Keira pointed out, her voice nearly drowned out by a peal of thunder that rattled the window panes, "but what about these caravans?"

Dymphna nodded absently, reaching for a tiny pair of scissors as her curtain of blond hair slid forward to hide her face. Keira was starting to regret telling the other girl about her training. She had known that Dymphna was less than comfortable with magic, but these days, she kept her eyes glued to her work whenever Keira was around. It stung, but at least she never brought it up or asked her to leave.

The three of them were sitting on cushions on the floor of Dymphna's room, trying to get through a mountain of work that would take three times as long as what had been allotted. But, when one was maid to a Duchess, questioning the work load wasn't really an option. Keira understood that, even if Arielle had ranted about it before dragging her here. It was one of the first times she had seen her friend truly angry.

Dymphna's rooms were a lot smaller than Keira's. It was little more than a bedchamber and water closet, but her friend had made the best of them. She had decorated her rooms in daisy yellow and white. Against the dark stone of the castle walls, it produced a warm and cheerful effect. She had even draped a white sheet across the dark ceiling, chasing away the chill and making it seem like a light and airy space, a style of decorating that Dymphna said was gaining popularity in the west.

Keira and Arielle were helping Dymphna remove the lace from the collars of several of Duchess Duval's gowns, as that style was falling out of fashion. The mindless task allowed them plenty of room for conversation, and the young women could speak of little else beyond the rumors that were flying through the castle.

After a pause, Dymphna added, "The last three shipments to Fort Ravemar never made it there. Two of them were just food and blankets, that sort of stuff. I heard about it from my Aunt in Dove's Landing."

"What about the third shipment?" Keira asked.

"Two cartloads of Oaklyran bows." Arielle said, her voice soft. "Not exactly something anyone wants in the hands of bandits. There were some crossbows and a catapult too. Powerful weapons."

"What's being done about it?" Keira asked, laying aside a large piece of lace.

"Nothing, as far as I know." Arielle shook her head.

"What *can* be done?" Dymphna asked, moving on to the next dress. "It's not as if they were even attacked in the same area. How is anyone supposed to track the raiders?"

"Do you think it's bandits or Eimar? I've heard some things that make me wonder." Arielle asked in a hushed tone.

"I don't think it's really band-ow!" Dymphna stopped to suck her pricked finger.

Keira held her hand out, "Here, let me?"

Dymphna's eyes widened and she went pale as she shook her head vehemently. "I don't need any healing."

"You don't want to bleed on Duchess Duval's lace." Keira

huffed and reached into her pocket to pull out a clean linen bandage. "No magic, I promise. Master Declan would kill me if I did any magical healing without his supervision anyway."

"Right. Sorry." She had the grace to blush. When Keira had finished bandaging the finger, Dymphna tossed her long hair over her shoulder and gestured at the pile of finished dresses. "It's really kind of you two to help me with this."

"I enjoy it." Keira said with a smile, "Besides, Duchess Duval probably thinks you're the best maid ever – somehow doing the work of three."

"Duchess Duval has other things on her mind. It's why she's been loading us with work lately. Normally, she's very in tune with how hard her maids are working."

"What's going on? Fionn hasn't mentioned anything." Keira's brow furrowed with concern.

"Oh no, it's nothing like that. Just a rumor about the queen that she has been doing her best to quash."

"What rumor?" Arielle asked, straightening her spine.

Keira laughed at her defensive posture. "Queen Olivia is human, even if she is royal."

"She is human." Arielle acknowledged, "but she has more enemies than most. Women who are jealous that they weren't chosen to wed the King."

"Enemies don't normally start rumors."

"Ha!" Arielle barked an uncharacteristically loud laugh.

"No, normally they'd set fires." Dymphna said, then clapped a hand over her mouth.

"What??" Her friends chorused.

"Just more rumors. Countess Le Brouch was seen in the market square the day of the fire."

"Are you sure? Was she visiting someone?"

"That's just it. Duchess Duval thought she saw her, but no one else did."

Keira sighed, "This is too much. I hope nothing worse is coming." The storm chose that moment to unleash another loud rumble, one that Keira felt vibrating up through the floor. *Dramatic, much?* She sighed.

Dymphna shrugged. "All of this is mere rumor."

"What was being said about the queen?" Arielle asked again, back still too straight.

"That she was seeing Councilor Stedman....privately."

Arielle went pale. "Impossible."

"It's just a rumor." Dymphna said firmly, "I don't believe it either."

"I hope this doesn't get back to Their Majesties." Keira breathed, "They don't need that with everything else that's been going on."

"What are you talking about?" Arielle asked, picking at a new thread.

"A couple of local patrols have been attacked. They got off alright, but never saw their attacker. One of the guards came in with an arrow wound. Declan and I healed him. Well...Declan healed him while I mostly watched."

"That's not good." Dymphna said flatly.

Keira shrugged. "They think it's a bold group of bandits."

"I take it back." Dymphna sighed. "There's *nothing* silly about it. The roads are frightful, and of course the stables are empty."

"I hope I didn't make a mistake taking the king's coin." Keira said in a small voice, "I don't want to be called on to hurt anyone."

Arielle assured her that it was unlikely, even if they went to war. She was a woman, and male ArKen were usually the only one's conscripted.

"And healers are valuable," Dymphna soothed.

But it did nothing to settle the uncomfortable feeling in the pit of her stomach.

Nine

Keira walked beside her parents, fidgeting nervously as they approached the manor house. The Duval's had a home in Ravenfell, in addition to their greater holdings in Rothkov and north of Ravenfell, and it was there that they were hosting their youngest son's birthday soirée. Keira felt self-conscious in the beautiful dress that was far too fancy for her and not nearly fancy enough for this party. Her father seemed to feel no such discomfort. He practically strutted in his best suit of clothes, polished boots gleaming.

"Aren't you nervous?" She whispered, slipping her hand through his free elbow. The other had naturally been claimed by her mother.

"Not really." He chuckled. "You're still young, but your mother and I used to attend this sort of event once in a while. You get used to them. Besides, the only thing you have to worry about is your shoes. They know it's a mixed bunch and as long as your shoes are presentable, no one will mind if your ears don't sparkle."

"Well, your father's not wrong." Her mother gave her a mischievous wink.

She swallowed hard against a nervous knot in her throat and looked down at the soft cloth shoes her father had bought her.

They were pink to match the dress, with tiny beads of pink glass to coordinate with her cracked rose necklace. They were beautiful, but left her feeling exposed. Keira couldn't help but wish that she had her comfortable boots instead of the flimsy cloth. A pearl hairpin that her mother had lent her glinted above her right ear, and Keira had to admit — she did feel beautiful.

It was lucky they were able to ride in a public carriage with several other invitees who also did not keep their own. Keira would have been perfectly content riding, but not in this dress. She could feel every tiny stone under her feet, but the walk from the carriage was mercifully short. They soon found themselves at the door.

The Duval's manor was in much the same style as the other homes in the city, but on a larger scale. The exterior walls were gray, with wooden beams crisscrossing across them in a pleasing pattern. The front garden was enchanting. It was small, simply framing the fence-enclosed courtyard. Instead of flowers, a variety of greenery occupied the beds. Ferns lined one wall, and there was a dizzying array of mosses arranged in small dry pools and spilling over the edge of a waterless fountain.

Keira smiled at the arrangement. She could feel magic in the garden, although it was subtle. Most probably would have missed it, even if it 'intersected their own power', as her master had put it. As she examined the working, it suddenly occurred to her to wonder if other Naturals could sense magic the way she could. She filed that away as another question to research in the library, now that she felt free to explore any book she chose.

Keira pulled her attention back to the present as they were shown into a gorgeous ballroom, one that was only made more beautiful by the party guests in all their finery. A long table, covered in white cloth, hugged one wall. Little cakes and other hors d'ouevres were arranged along the table, with painted porcelain plates too small to satisfy a bird's appetite. Every surface was draped in white silk and gauzy linen in the same color. Above the guests, two enormous crystal chandeliers threw little bits of rainbow light across the whole room. A great tapestry covered the far wall from floor to ceiling. It depicted an old-fashioned hunt, of the sort that had gone out of fashion in recent years, as they were dangerous and not a little cruel.

Keira was surprised to see the weaving. She had never thought of tapestries as decorations for ballrooms. She supposed it was flat enough that the musicians would be able to be heard despite the acoustics. *Then again, perhaps it was necessary given the number of musicians that had been hired.* The sound of them tuning their instruments was loud enough as it drifted over the heads of the party guests who continued to trickle in. It would be even louder when all dozen played in unison.

"We should greet our hosts," Keira's pa said, interrupting her ogling.

"Right." She wrenched her attention away from the decorations and followed her pa toward Duchess Duval and her son.

"Where is the duke?" She whispered.

"Oh, I doubt he's here. Their main estate is pretty far away, and things are a little unsettled in that region."

"Oh." Keira was glad she had asked before they reached the pair at the other end of the ballroom.

Duchess Duval looked divine in an ice blue gown. The cut showed off her figure, which was very fine for a woman her age, without appearing to sacrifice modesty. The fabric must have been satin, and lace covered a large portion of her sleeves. Small diamonds glinted at her ears and throat.

She greeted them warmly, and her son stepped forward to do the same. "Welcome, I hope you enjoy the party." Fionn said, smoothing his dark blue doublet.

"Thank you." Keira curtsied as her father bowed. She hoped her blush didn't show, but she suspected that her face matched her dress. *He's so handsome.*

"How did the exam go?" Fionn asked.

Keira grinned. "I passed."

He turned to the next guest as they moved away. The musicians started playing before long, though nobody danced. Everyone gathered in small groups to make smaller talk, while Keira wandered the edge of the room looking for a face she knew. Her parents had gone to greet another smith and his wife.

"Dymphna!" Keira exclaimed when she nearly bumped into her. "You blend right in!"

"All the servants are wearing white." Dymphna explained. "That way we don't clash, and if someone needs help they can find us quickly."

It was a testament to how much white silk and linen was draped around the ballroom that a pure white outfit should blend in.

"Another color might have stood out more." She finally said.

Dymphna snorted. "Probably."

The two didn't have much time to chat before Dymphna was called away to her duties. Keira had never been to a party like this and didn't really know what to do with herself. She continued to wander the edges and when she was certain that people were, in fact, eating she got herself a snack.

She found herself standing next to Master Elers when the dancing started.

"Having a nice time?" he asked, as Fionn opened the dance with a party guest in a brown dress adorned with small glittering stones.

"It's a beautiful party." She said, ignoring the twinge of jealousy she felt as she watched them twirl around the dance floor.

"That's not what I asked." He shrugged. "Parties aren't my favorite either."

"I'm glad I was invited." She hedged.

"Me too, of course. Fionn is my closest friend and I'm always happy to celebrate with him. But I think we'll have more fun sharing a drink after."

Keira smiled. "That sounds nice."

They stood for a while watching the dancers move on to new partners as the music shifted. She sighed. *They really are a lovely sight*. The men stood tall and moved sedately as the women swirled around them. Keira wished she might join them, but no one asked her. After a while, Declan went to get them drinks. Keira sipped her punch cautiously. It looked like it would stain. It was very good, however. She enjoyed hers rather quickly, and when Fionn joined them he passed her empty cup to Declan.

"Do you like dancing?" He asked, his amber-green eyes twinkling.

"No one has asked. I don't know if I'd like it."

"You don't know." He blinked in surprise, then pointed skyward in an imitation of a famous naturalist. "Then we must experiment. May I have this dance?"

She grinned. "Certainly. If it's in the pursuit of knowledge."

He winked and took her hand, leading her out onto the dance floor. Keira was nervous, and a bit lightheaded as he placed one hand on her waist and wrapped his other hand gently around hers. The way her heart raced and her breathing sped up at his touch was unreasonable and entirely unfair, but no matter what she told herself, her body would not comply.

As the music rose to a crescendo around them, she discovered that she loved dancing with him. Fionn's hand was incredibly warm and his eyes sparkled with good humor as he pulled her around the dance floor. The music was a bit too fast for any real conversation, but that suited her fine at the moment. Her mouth was dry and her heart raced more than the dancing could account for.

She was a bit breathless by the time she swirled with the other ladies and traded partners momentarily. When they traded back she was greeted by a grin just for her. She smiled back, and the pair continued to rotate partners as the music sped. Finally, it was time to return to the first steps of the dance. Keira worried she would trip, but her feet felt light in her new slippers. She was still grinning as they returned, hand in hand, to Declan's side.

"Who is *that*?" She heard a woman in green ask another.

"I think she came in with one of the blacksmiths," the other woman said with a sniff.

Keira tried not to let it bother her. She had to remind herself that she was no longer just a blacksmith's daughter. As an ArKen, she had every right to stand beside two noble sons at a party. It might take a while for her to feel it, but that was the truth. A new world would open to her as she pursued her training.

She did her best to keep up with Fionn's and Declan's conversation, which was mostly focused on their horses. This was something she could engage in enthusiastically, a favorite topic of her own.

She thought of Cinnamon in his stall and smiled to herself. Dymphna had exercised him while her hands were injured, without her ever having to ask. She simply noticed that she hadn't ridden him and took care of it. Even though the pair were not really on comfortable footing at the time, it was a kindness that she appreciated, when she finally learned of it.

It did not fit into the conversation, however. Instead, the men were debating breeding lines. Keira knew very little of the subtopic. Fionn seemed particularly well informed and she told him so, blushing furiously. He took the time from gushing about his new mount to tell her a little context for why he was so excited. From what she could gather, he was basically a hybrid of a domestic warhorse and an imported racer.

"That sounds like a lot of horse." She mumbled.

"His temper is good, if he's a bit energetic."

"My parents' mule is gentle as a lamb." Keira sighed happily. "He tolerates noises well, and his gait is smooth enough to shoot from."

"You do mounted archery?" Fionn asked in surprise.

Keira shrugged. "Some, but I haven't had much practice. I certainly couldn't keep up with the soldiers."

"But you don't have a horse of your own?" If any other noble had asked the question, it might have held judgment, but the only thing in Fionn's voice was surprise. And he grimaced as soon as he said it.

She sighed and opened her mouth to answer him, but she nearly threw up instead as the room seemed to buckle around her. There was a discordant buzzing filling the air, although Keira was aware that she wasn't *hearing* it in the traditional sense. It felt like magic, but not like magic at all. The magic she had sensed up until this point felt like a natural part of the world, something that simply was. This felt like something that shouldn't be.

Keira looked up to see Fionn's face frozen in horror. She smelled the smoke before she turned around. The great tapestry had caught fire. She couldn't imagine how, since there were no candles near it. *Unless someone used magic.* Maybe this was what her magic had felt like to others, before she had any control of it.

The fire was spreading quickly. It seemed that whatever fabric had been draped over everything was highly flammable. Within half a minute, the tables and window coverings were burning. *How is it spreading so fast? Does fire always do that?* Two ladies' dresses caught, and the ballroom devolved into a cacophony of screams and breaking glassware. A gentleman grabbed the punch bowl and dumped it on one of the ladies' skirts. The fire went out, blessedly. But it did not relieve the greater fire, that threatened them all.

Fionn looked on in horror and Declan simply stared.

"Can you help?" Keira asked her new teacher.

He shook his head. "I've never been able to control fire."

The screams got louder as the fire spread. Most of the other guests were running towards the doors, but a second fire had started on that side of the room, and it blocked them in.

Keira took a few steps, then turned to Declan. "Is my knowledge of fire accurate?"

"What?" He asked stupidly.

"Is my understanding of fire accurate? You spent the better part of an hour testing me on chemical changes last week."

"Yes. You know fire, but..." He fell silent as Keira closed her already glowing eyes.

She bent her knees slightly and then drew her hands up in a wave-like motion, pulling the currents of her power down her arms and out towards the fire. She could feel it spread through the whole ballroom, and touch the flames. She took a deep breath, and when she released it a wave of cold spread out from her.

It left a trail of frost in its wake, but Keira ignored that. Her frost did not quench the fire of human bodies. She made sure of that. Instead, she found the flames that were licking at the walls, the tapestry, curtains, and even three of the voluminous skirts the noble women preferred.

Once the fire had been quenched, Keira brought her hands back down in front of her, pressing them towards the floor. She opened her gleaming silver eyes and they faded to a dull gray. She was surprised to see an icy wind settle at the attendees feet, but gratified that there was no longer any trace of fire. She shivered.

Every eye in the ballroom was on her. Keira took another deep breath and it hung like fog in the air as she released it. She noticed that no one else breathed fog. The air temperature seemed to be returning to a comfortable level, but she was still freezing. She looked down to find her sleeves coated in frost, and then over at Master Declan, a question on her face.

He had no answer, instead staring at her mutely, just like everyone else.

"Who is *that*?" She heard a woman whisper to her neighbor.

The ballroom filled with the cumulative clamor of a hundred whispers. Absurdly, Keira looked down at the frost coating her dress and laughed. She couldn't help it. The sound seemed to break the moment, and Duchess Duval swept forward, embracing her.

"Oh — no, Your Grace." Keira pulled back. "I haven't quite warmed up."

Duchess Duval stepped back, shivering.

Shaking himself, Declan grabbed Keira by the shoulders and

led her through a mental exercise which brought her back to room temperature.

"Thank you." She whispered urgently, quiet enough no one else could hear.

"We owe you our thanks." Duchess Duval said in a loud, carrying voice. "You have saved us all, Mistress Smith."

"I haven't earned that title." Keira hedged. "I just started training."

"Then I expect we shall see great things from you, Apprentice Smith." She smiled warmly.

Nobody else looked very friendly. She saw uneasiness in Elers' eyes and looked no further. Keira couldn't look at Fionn. She was afraid to see it there too.

Was it that impressive? I only stopped a simple fire. It was large, to be sure, but it wasn't as though she had regrown someone's nerves. It was odd that she had spread frost though. The heat had been smothered by her magic and she wasn't entirely sure where the energy had gone. That wasn't how heat worked. But Keira was too confused to say anything before her parents stepped forward to usher her out of the ballroom.

* * *

That night Keira sat wrapped in a blanket on her living room couch, already changed into her nightclothes and with a mug of deliciously warm drinking chocolate cradled in her fingers. Her mother sat next to her, sipping her own portion of the luxurious drink. Keira briefly wondered where her papa had procured it, but the look on his face brought her attention back to the conversation at hand.

He leaned forward in his chair and rested his chin on his folded hands. "I had no idea you were capable of...so much."

"It wasn't that much. *Really.*" Keira insisted as his eyebrows rose. "It was simple. I'm a Natural, father. I have plenty of power, just not the knowledge to use it."

The conversation had long since turned circular. Keira must have explained this four or five times. She stared glumly at the pink and blue floral rug at her feet.

Her mother rubbed gentle circles into her back. "You must have been frightened?"

Keira nodded. "You were there. The ballroom was chaos."

"I meant using your magic like that." Her mother set her chocolate aside to give Keira a squeeze.

"That part was easy," Keira said softly.

"How is that possible?" Her father asked.

"I just said- " Keira started.

"You don't understand, Sprout. What you did was *nowhere* close to normal. I've never seen such a display of power, and I grew up with your Aunt Rose. She's considered strong, even for a Natural."

"From what I understand...magic requires knowledge of the thing manipulated. Knowledge and energy. Naturals have energy, and I've been doing all that reading. I think you're overestimating how much power this took." She set her empty mug on a side table. "*Causing* a fire like that would have been much more demanding."

"Maybe," He shook his head as if disagreeing with himself.

Her mother hugged her tighter and murmured into her hair. "My little Keira. Please be careful."

"I will. I *am*."

"We'll have to call you Mistress from now on." Her father joked.

Keira stuck her tongue out.

"What lovely manners, Mistress Sprout." He leaned back to grab his now cold drinking chocolate from the table where he'd abandoned it and gave a heavy sigh. "Well, things are going to change for us. Quietly training is one thing, but you're going to be the talk of the kingdom for a while."

Keira privately disagreed. *With all the things happening in Ravena, why would anyone care about one apprentice ArKen?*

Ten

Keira left her apartment as soon as the light filtering through the windows was enough to see by. She knew that Declan was an early riser, and she had *questions*. And no doubt, he'd have some too. She sighed, eyes darting between doorways as she walked. Keira might disagree with her parents that she would be 'the talk of the kingdom', but that didn't mean she wanted to meet any of the other castle residents at the moment.

When Keira reached Declan's clinic, she was surprised to find a few lights already floating in the waiting room. It was pretty early, even for Declan. She rolled her shoulders and headed for the inner office. She paused halfway through the door, her hand raised to announce herself with a knock on the frame. Declan wasn't alone. Selene sat with him, sipping from a porcelain teacup. Her black hair was thrown up in a messy bun, but she appeared otherwise ready for the day.

"Keira." Selene greeted her warmly, "I didn't expect to find you here this early."

"Nor I." Keira acknowledged. "I hope you're having a good morning."

"So far." She looked around the room, then set her tea down on the edge of the desk. "Do you smell smoke?"

Declan gestured to the remaining chair and Keira took it. She grimaced. "That's probably me. I couldn't get the smell out of my hair."

"And why should your hair smell like smoke?" She asked, as if it were an everyday question.

"There was a fire at the Duval manor yesterday."

"I did hear. I hope no one was harmed?"

Keira shook her head.

"That's lucky. Your master has been telling me that you tried your hand at fire-control."

"I....put it out." Keira acknowledged reluctantly.

She didn't like the uneasiness she had seen in others, but Selene didn't show a trace of it as she answered with a laugh, "It's fortunate you were there. Quite the display of power from our little Natural, if the fire was indeed large enough to trap the guests."

"So I'm told. It didn't seem that impressive to me." Keira sighed, glancing at Declan.

He nodded encouragingly.

"Of course not. You wouldn't realize how little power most Seekers manage to unlock. I wouldn't be able to put out a fire larger than the one in my hearth....come to think of it, that would be rather difficult..." She trailed off, staring into space.

"Mistress Selene?" Keira prompted.

Selene came back to Earth and met her intense gaze.

"Do either of you know why I would be cold afterward?" Keira's fingers absently traced the embossed letters of a book that sat on Declan's desk. It must have been popular. Arielle was gushing about it the week before.

Selene leaned forward, "Hmm....that depends what you did. I'm rather curious actually. The human body gets its energy from what is essentially a slow fire. How did you differentiate?"

Keira shrugged. "People have sort of a natural barrier. I was careful not to cross it."

"A natural barrier? Do you mean their skin?" Selene frowned. "I don't see why that would help."

Keira shook her head. "Not skin. I don't know what to call it."

Selene's eyes widened. "Can you sense other people's latent magic?"

"Anyone can sense magic, when it intersects their own," Declan explained. "It means that Keira has been paying attention to her lessons on healing."

While he was talking, Selene filled another teacup with water, heating it in a moment and adding a small pouch of tea leaves. She passed it to Keira. "I suspect the reason you were cold is simply because you used a great deal of power. That energy had to come from somewhere."

Keira put a lump of sugar in her tea while Selene spread white cheese on a thick slice of bread for each of them. She thought about what Selene had said. *So, there are natural limitations on how much magic I can use.* Keira pondered that, but wondered if it was merely a matter of speed, rather than the magic itself. Her true limitation might be physical.

"Why did my dress and the floor around me get icy?" She asked, taking a sip of the fresh tea.

"They did?" Declan asked, his eyebrows drawing together in a look he only got when he was doing his most serious thinking.

Keira nodded.

"That *is* interesting." Selene said thoughtfully as she took her own sip of tea. "It may be that the moisture in the air settled and froze. Like an accelerated form of dew frost."

"That would make sense." Keira agreed slowly.

They fell into silence as they all processed their own thoughts. Keira's silence lasted longer, while Selene and Declan chatted about the play between temperature and moisture in the ballroom. Their exchange ended with Selene's book being added to Keira's curriculum.

When they fell silent, Keira asked her most important question, "What limits a person's magic?"

Declan was silent for long enough Keira began to wonder if he would answer.

Selene stood with a slight curtsy for Declan and a nod for Keira. "This is a conversation for master and apprentice. Besides, I have a mountain of work to get through today. We'll chat another time."

Silence filled the room again as the door fell closed with a soft *thump*.

"Master?"

"You've asked a question with an unknown answer," Declan said finally, chewing his words as though they could jump out and bite them. "For most of us, it seems to be a matter of physical energy. Naturals run on something different."

"How so?"

"I have no idea where you get your energy. It seems like the only real limitation for Naturals is how swiftly they can channel their magic, and that varies wildly. There are a few stories of your kind tiring after a long day of silver work, but mostly it's just a chill."

Keira nodded.

But Declan's voice shifted into something more serious, "The silver chill can kill. If I had known what you were planning, I would have urged caution."

"I *was* cautious."

He frowned and gave a slow shake of his head. "There's no way that anyone could burn that much power that quickly while being careful."

Keira shifted uncomfortably in her seat. The truth was, she hadn't been careful. If she had paused a moment to think, she might not have acted. Since no one had died, and few had been injured, she couldn't bring herself to regret her recklessness. It was also the thing that told her how different she was from the average ArKen. Most people understood the limits of an ArKen, but Keira had no frame of reference. The ArKen she knew the most of was her Aunt, but she was a Natural too, by all accounts a powerful one.

"I will grant that you were not *entirely* reckless. It was a good thing that you paused to verify your understanding, but we'll need to find your limits, for your own safety. You did well, Kei. You saved lives by acting so quickly, mine included."

"Thank you, Master."

* * *

The next day, Keira woke to a persistent tapping on her door. *It can't be morning already.* She stood with a groan and stumbled over to look out the window, lifting the velvet curtain aside. It was gray, and a persistent wind made the sparse raindrops loud. Dawn must have been at *least* an hour or two away.

The knock came again, and Keira hastened to wrap a blanket around herself. She didn't have a robe, something she promised herself she would correct now that she had an income that didn't need stretching. The knock came again, and this time Keira was awake enough to worry.

In an almost reflexive reaction, she unfurled her magic to see who was at her door. It was only Declan, and he seemed perfectly relaxed, eyes half-lidded as he covered a yawn with one of the steaming mugs he had in each hand. Keira breathed a sigh of relief. If someone was hurt, there would be more urgency. Still, she hurried to the door.

"Get dressed." Declan handed her one of the mugs. "We have a lot of work to do."

Keira looked down into the clay mug and found a black liquid. It had a pleasant smell, but not one that was particularly appetizing. "What's this?"

"Coffee. Drink up. You'll be shadowing me today and I keep long hours."

It was the same drink that Arielle's parents sometimes indulged in when they were feeling homesick. Keira had heard of it only because Mrs. Black missed it now she was pregnant. Keira sipped experimentally at the cup and grimaced, then gagged. It was bitter enough to taste like poison and acidic enough to make her worry about her teeth. *Why would anyone drink this willingly?*

"Your loss." Declan said with a laugh, reclaiming her mug and downing it in one swig.

Keira's eyes widened. It was clearly too hot to drink that fast, but Declan didn't seem to notice.

"Go on." He bounced on the balls of his feet, a teasing smile on his lips. "Lots to do."

The door closed in her face. Keira blinked. Then she groaned and got dressed, still rubbing the sleep from her eyes. When she opened her front door for the second time, she was wearing a belted green dress with her leather vest tugged firmly over it. Declan was free of the mugs, and still too energetic for this time of the morning.

She let out a long suffering sigh, but hurried to keep up as he led the way through the dark castle corridors. There were no windows after the first corridor, but when it got too dark, Declan opened his palm and a globe light appeared. Keira eyed it with a twinge of jealousy, quickly squashed by fear. She was glad Declan hadn't tried to teach her to make them yet. She didn't know when she'd be ready, but the thought of another attempt sent an unpleasant shiver down her spine and into her hands.

The castle looked so different in the dark that Keira was caught by surprise when their journey ended at the library. She looked up to find a few pale, fading orbs of light drifting near the lofty ceiling, barely visible. Without the sea of lights that was usually suspended there, the library was transformed.

The bright colors of the carpet and chairs were muted and

shadows pooled in unexpected places, making the library seem more like a darkened forest. The whisper of magic from the remnants of the orbs that usually bobbed around the ceiling only served to emphasize the intense silence.

A sharp crack made Keira whirl around to face her master.

He drew his hands apart. "Let's get started, shall we?"

Keira stared at him stupidly and he pointed at the ceiling. *Drat.*

"Follow me and observe the first few times." Declan instructed.

Keira obediently followed his work with her mind. It seemed simple, watching him as he drew a thread of his power and transformed it into a cherry red orb of light, which he released to float upward. He repeated the process several more times, shifting ever so slightly as he produced one of a soft blue. The next was almost the same shade of sunshine yellow as Keira's first disastrous attempt. Declan hadn't witnessed that, so she knew he hadn't intended to remind her, but she recoiled all the same.

Unfortunately, he noticed.

"What is it?"

"What if it happens again?" Keira rubbed her left palm with her opposite thumb, fighting a sudden stinging behind her eyes.

"It won't. Your problem was never control and you know better now. I have complete confidence in you."

"I don't," Keira admitted, but she took a deep breath and set her feet.

Still unprepared, she took another and closed her eyes. She tried to remember what it had felt like, to access her power that first time, then decided that was a terrible idea and opened her eyes again.

"Kei, come on. I know you can do this. Most ArKen can and you're extraordinarily gifted."

She nodded. He was right, she knew that this wasn't a complicated task. Her breath hitched as she concentrated on the point between her shaking hands. Ever so carefully, Keira let her power flow into it. Slowly, almost painfully so, a heatless orb of light appeared. It was the size and color of a ripe apricot, and she couldn't help but cheer as she sent it drifting toward the ceiling.

"Well done." Declan set a hand on her shoulder. "Let's make the next one a little larger."

Keira let out a shaky laugh. "As you say."

The next half hour was spent in the same way, filling every inch of the ceiling with light. After a few minutes, her hands stopped shaking and she started enjoying herself. They didn't discuss a color scheme, but most of the lights Declan made were red and yellow, with a handful of blue orbs to balance them. And there was just something about the autumn season that made Keira want to match the foliage. She experimented with colors. Some of hers were a bright orange, some a soft beige, but most were two or three colors in one. By the time they finished, the atmosphere in the library was warmer than usual — the kind of soft light that made you want to curl up with a mug of tea and read your favorite book by a fire.

Despite the earliness of the hour, and the difficulty of overcoming her fear, the first hour of the day was the easiest. After the library, Keira followed Declan back to his office. She filled his waiting room with light without his assistance, and then the real work started.

Declan's first patient of the day was a kitchen maid with a burn on her forearm. After asking her permission, Declan instructed Keira to follow along. She did so, but it turned her stomach to see burns like that in another person. She suspected burns would always be difficult for her. She bolstered Declan's strength with her own, allowing him to heal the mark completely.

The next patient surprised Keira. One of the local farmers arrived. She wasn't sure what was wrong with him at first, other than a fever. His skin was mottled and his eyes glassy, but he didn't seem sick enough to seek help. Then, he pulled up his pant leg to reveal the dirtiest bandage Keira had ever seen. And when it was removed, Keira only avoided gagging at the smell by using her magic to temporarily suppress her own gag reflex.

That was only the beginning. Patient after patient sought Declan's help. Every patient was methodically evaluated in the exact same manner — a process Keira soon memorized. She was surprised by how rarely her master actually used magic. Most patients received an herbal remedy or a simple bandage. Many had magic applied to speed the beginning of their healing, but Declan left their bodies to finish the work.

Between patients, he explained that he would run out of magic if he used it on everyone. Keira could see that he was right. Between mixing medicines, boiling bandages, and healing patients, she was physically exhausted by the time clinic hours ended. She had magic to spare — lots of it, she suspected — but Declan was a Seeker, not a Natural. And still he managed to heal everyone who really needed it.

Keira couldn't help admiring his work ethic. There were few noble sons, even third sons, who would be on call for a stable hand or the farmers and merchants who frequented his clinic. She couldn't have found a better person to learn healing from. Despite her exhaustion, she went to bed with her heart full.

* * *

As autumn faded into winter, the rumors swirling around the kingdom seemed to die down. People traveled more, first because they couldn't wait any longer to sell their goods, and then because it seemed safe. One shipment of supplies went missing, along with the handful of guards who accompanied it, but it was put down to a bad storm in the forest. A tragedy, to be sure, but not something to worry over.

Keira's studies continued as the season shifted, and true to his word, Declan did his best to test her limits. Now allowed to shadow him in the clinic, she added her power to his. Normally, he reserved magical healing for serious injuries, but for weeks, he had Keira heal even the most superficial of wounds. He claimed it was good experience for her, but from the way he questioned her every hour, it seemed like he had a secondary motive. She never tired, and the chills did not return. But she did gain enough experience that Declan allowed her to heal simple injuries without supervision.

On a snowy day, he took Keira outside and set her to monitoring several fires. She was to maintain them at various temperatures and colors — red, orange, yellow, white, and blue. This proved more challenging at first, but once she had a feel for each temperature range, it became simple. It was more tiring to stand there all morning than it was to keep the fires at the specified temperature.

For Midwinter, Declan set her loose in the castle. She was to decorate the entire place with globe lights, and any other magical ornaments she could devise. The creative freedom was unexpected, but it came with a lecture on caution — and required a promise that she would return to his office if, at any time, she felt the slightest chill, or if she grew sleepy.

So, Keira wandered the castle for several days, releasing tiny globe lights into every nook and cranny she could find. Some of them were bright, while others were nearly invisible. After some experimentation, Keira managed to produce tiny, glittery effects, as well as silvery whorls that she had fun sprinkling around the walls and ceiling of the king's dining hall. After purchasing her latest stack of books, it felt nice to do something special for the royal family. Her decoration mission lasted eight hours a day for six days in a row, but the only tiredness Keira felt was from walking. The decorations only lasted a day or two, as was typical of globe lights. After that, Declan wore his thinking face for a solid week and his tests stopped.

Shortly after Midwinter, Keira got to help deliver Arielle's baby brother. It was a smooth delivery, and the family welcomed little Beau with nothing but joy. The change in Arielle was palpable. As the delivery had grown closer, dark circles had appeared under her eyes and she had lost weight. Thankfully, after her brother was born, it was rare to see her without a smile.

Keira started her third unit of study as winter melted into spring. The texts she poured over now were considerably more advanced, but she found most of them fascinating. Still, as the days grew muddy and she spent more time indoors, it began to feel like all she did was study. Her one consolation was that her friends and family were often happy to sit with her while she did it, either working on a project of their own, or during one of their breaks. Somehow, studying was always more fun when Fionn was around. He introduced her to the concept of flashcards, and it was a game changer. Declan's exams seemed less overwhelming after that.

* * *

It rained for two weeks straight in the middle of spring. Keira wouldn't have minded, if it wasn't for the unseasonable cold. Rain wasn't unusual, of course, but the way it never stopped was. Nobody else complained, but she was so cold at times that she felt nauseous.

She retreated under mountains of blankets to study, and used some of her new income to purchase more drinking chocolate. Tonight, she was cocooned on a couch in Arielle's rooms. Arielle was alternating between writing a library report for the crown and cooing at little Beau. Dymphna had brought some of her sewing along.

Dymphna broke a long silence that had been punctuated only by the sound of thread-picking, "I can't believe the guard still hasn't caught the person who set the fires."

"That's if they weren't an accident." Arielle disagreed gently.

"Don't be naive," Keira chided. She let her book fall closed and shoved it off her lap.

"You two are from the countryside. You don't realize how bad a fire can be in the city. It doesn't mean it was anything nefarious."

"Maybe not," Keira conceded. "But I keep hearing talk of spies."

"Talk is probably all it is." Dymphna said as she started to repair a small rip in a stocking.

"My pa has heard interesting rumors among the other smiths, although I suspect it's all second-hand from customers. But they do supply most of the weapons that the guard uses, so it could be that the gossip in the smithy is accurate."

"Well, we can comfort ourselves that if there *are* spies, they aren't very good ones," Arielle said with a shrug. "There haven't been any problems in months."

Keira reached for a gown from Dymphna's pile.

"I'm to remove the lace collar. Nobody wears them anymore."

"Are we removing lace on the sleeves as well?" Keira held it up.

Dymphna glanced up from her work. "Not on the bell sleeves. Queen Olivia loves her dragging sleeves and Duchess Duval loves anything the queen does. At least my lady's sleeves don't drag on the floor." Dymphna pulled a face. "I imagine the queen's household need to repair her gowns constantly. Nobody is that graceful, not even royalty."

"I'm sure she is," Arielle said, almost to herself.

"Perhaps." Dymphna smirked. "But my lady is practical."

They fell silent, except for Arielle cooing at her brother.

"The duchess mentioned that you've been spending a lot of time with her son lately." Dymphna's lips twitched in a knowing smile.

Keira felt her face go hot at the same time as her pulse ratcheted up. *If Duchess Duval thinks I'm setting my cap at her son...the lowly daughter of a blacksmith — magic or no, I wouldn't dare.*

"A good reading buddy is difficult to come by," Arielle said in the same sing-song voice she had been using with her brother, making a silly face at the baby.

It was hard to tell if she meant to tease her, so Keira didn't answer. She shifted, stretching her legs straight in front of herself. A change of subject was for the best. "How long until the diplomats arrive?"

That was the latest piece of news — diplomats from Eimar were to visit and discuss some sort of trade deal. The servants were saying that they weren't invited, but that didn't make much difference to Keira's mind. One kingdom or the other had to initiate diplomacy.

"Two weeks." Arielle replied in a baby voice, making a goofy face for the baby.

"It has *been* two weeks for the last month." Dymphna harrumphed.

"Well, the weather hasn't been good. It's difficult to travel through muck," Arielle hedged.

"We'll see. If they came through the forest, that would certainly explain it." Dymphna shuddered. "No one should travel through Gyre Forest. The southern road is much safer."

Nobody disagreed.

Keira plucked the lace from the collars of two of Duchess Duval's gowns before returning to her studies. The newest round of reading had brought with it a renewed focus of learning and Keira was not so sure she liked it. Chemical science seemed designed to confuse, although whenever Declan spoke of it, he grew animated in a way that she had rarely seen. It was unfortunate that her least favorite subject should be one of her master's favorites, but at least it motivated her to study harder.

Eleven

Two weeks later, Keira sat at a table in the library, her eyes blurring and her head swimming as she read the same paragraph for the eighth time. If possible, the passage made even *less* sense than it had on her first read-through. She dropped her elbows on the table and closed her eyes, digging her fingers into her eyelids with a muffled groan.

"That's your cue to take a break."

Keira jumped as Fionn plopped a basket on the table, then her stomach flipped pleasantly as he leaned closer.

He met her eyes. "Join me for lunch?"

She snorted and snapped the book shut. "Yeah, okay."

"That took convincing." Fionn lifted the basket higher than necessary and strode away with a mischievous glance over his shoulder.

Keira scrambled to collect her books and match his brisk pace, smiling at his good mood. By the time they dropped her books in her sitting room and made it outside, her mood matched his, her fruitless struggles with chemical science forgotten. The gentle warmth of the spring sun felt wonderful on her shoulders.

When Fionn took her hand to lead her down a root-strewn path in the woods, it felt like the most natural thing in the world.

It didn't occur to Keira that they were holding hands until the path smoothed out and he didn't let go. Her heart raced, but she didn't want to be the one to pull away. His hand was so warm.

They walked in silence with their hands joined for another ten minutes before the woods opened up into a sunlit glade. Fionn's hand finally slid from hers so he could reach into his oversized basket and retrieve a blanket. He spread it on the ground before gesturing for her to sit.

Keira was quick to comply. Fionn joined her and continued emptying the basket. He drew bread, cheese, cold meats, fruit, and wine from the basket before turning to her with a question in his eyes.

Keira looked down at her hands, folded in her lap. She realized then that most likely, she shouldn't have come out alone with him. It was foolish. Keira trusted Fionn with her life. She had no doubts about his character and knew that he would never intentionally hurt her reputation, but it wouldn't look good if they were seen.

"Do you ever get tired of studying?"

The lightness of the question relaxed her, and Keira forgot her worries for the moment. "It isn't that different from what I was doing before I came to Ravenstone Keep."

Fionn's eyebrows lifted with curiosity and he leaned toward her. "I can't believe I've never asked, but what were you doing before you joined us?"

"I was halfway through an unofficial apprenticeship, studying to be an herbalist and midwife."

Fionn's arm twitched in her direction and then stopped. His brows drew down. "Do you regret that you weren't able to complete that apprenticeship?"

Keira shook her head. She felt a small pang of nostalgia, but it was eclipsed by a warmth that made her smile. "I've always wanted to be a healer. In Stoneybrooke, I chose the best means I had. But as an ArKen, especially as Declan's apprentice, I'll be able to do so much more. I'm lucky I got this opportunity." She closed her eyes as the sun broke through the trees, pouring warmth and light onto her face.

She could hear the smile in Fionn's voice as he replied, "I'm glad. Sometimes I worry you might be unhappy, since you tried so hard to avoid training your magic."

"Things worked out for the best. I avoided my magic out of fear, not because I truly hated it. What about you? Do you have an ambition of that sort? Or- maybe that isn't something nobles think about..." Keira grimaced and turned to look at him again.

To her relief, Fionn snorted. "Some don't. But much like Declan, I'm a third son. I had to give it some thought, since if I ever inherit my father's title, then things have gone very *very* wrong."

Keira took a bite of her lunch, waiting for him to continue.

After a pause to drink, he did, "I don't have a natural talent, and I've never been the scholarly sort, so learning magic wasn't for me."

Keira frowned. "Do a lot of nobles study magic? Did you?"

Fionn gave a self-depreciating laugh. "It's popular enough among second sons. Declan and I were friends from our boyhood, so yeah...I gave it a go. But it was never right for me." He started on his own lunch.

Keira gave him a minute to chew, flicked an ant off their blanket, then returned her attention to Fionn's face. "Do you know what you'll do instead?"

"My father has given me the space I need to figure that out, and lately I've been experimenting with horse-breeding. I love the animals, and it's..." Fionn chewed on his cheek as he thought. "...it's something that I think will be useful. For my family, and for the kingdom at large."

"Your father?" Keira hated the way her body tensed at the reminder that Fionn was the son of a Duke.

"My father, of course. And my eldest brother, when he takes his place. But as long as I can sell some of them to other nobles, it should be profitable enough to comfortably support a wife and children. It's something I think about. Don't you want a family?"

The intensity in his eyes when he asked the question made Keira's heart do a somersault into her stomach. She couldn't look away as she answered, "I do. I think I'd be a good mother...a good wife, but..." She cleared her throat and looked away. "It isn't something I expect I'll get to have. As a Natural, my social position is so strange. I can't marry a peasant, and I can't imagine any noble family accepting a blacksmith's daughter as their own."

The silence was long and painful, but when Fionn's response came, his voice was gentle. "Don't give up on the possibility."

Keira looked up to meet his eyes, afraid of what she'd see. When there was no pity in them, she breathed a sigh of relief. Instead, there was something like determination there. His pupils dilated as he looked at her, shrinking his irises to thin amber rings around an inky pool. Keira wasn't sure what it meant, but it made her heart race and she was both relieved and disappointed when he finally looked away.

By the time they finished their lunch, any awkwardness Keira felt at her admission had been buried in laughter. Fionn might not see himself as a scholar, but he had a quick mind and a clever tongue.

Fionn held her hand on the return trip, claiming it long before the roots invaded their path. This time, her palms grew sweaty. *Is he courting me?* She didn't want to admit to herself how much she liked the thought.

* * *

The next afternoon, Keira sat under a tree at the edge of the castle courtyard. The road lay behind her, and a fountain burbled in the center of the garden, an overlarge statue of a unicorn prancing through the pool. Keira's legs were folded underneath her and her skirt was growing damp from the soft earth as she listened intensely to Declan's instructions. This was the first time he was really letting her experiment with her powers. The closest she had come was being permitted to play with lighting effects for Midwinter decorations. Her heart thudded as Declan spoke, and her mouth grew drier by the moment.

"We won't know where your gifts lie until you explore more schools of magic. You're doing well with healing, but some ArKen choose more than one specialization, and it seems likely, given your strength, that you would be among them."

She swallowed hard against the knot in her throat.

"So what are you going to try first?" He asked, grinning as he relaxed his posture.

"Making fog."

He coughed into his fist, Keira suspected to disguise a laugh. "An advanced choice."

"Is it?" She asked, surprised.

He shrugged. "From here on out, I'll be keeping my opinions to myself. However, if you find that something is too difficult or requires too much of your energy, stop immediately. Now, let's see some fog."

Keira nodded. For once, she didn't close her eyes, instead looking up at the clouds. It was colder up there, but she wasn't sure if that's all it would take. She shivered as the air near the ground condensed and cooled, aware that her eyes were shifting to a misty silver based on the pleasant warmth there. It was a humid day, so there was plenty of moisture to work with. Keira was pleased when a cloud of fog spread out from her seated form to blanket the courtyard in white. She grinned at Declan, but he didn't see because they were entirely obscured.

"Well done!" he exclaimed. "Can you dismiss it?"

Keira shivered, but slowly warmed up the air around them so that the fog dispersed.

"Wonderful! It seems that you're a natural weather-worker."

Keira smiled, "Thank you, Master." It had become rare for her to call Declan 'Master', but today felt like a significant milestone in her training.

"What's next?"

"I want to master fire."

"You've worked with fire before." Declan acknowledged.

Understatement of the year, Keira thought with a grimace, flashing back to Fionn's party, although she suspected Declan was referring to her winter training session.

"In this case, I urge extra caution. I cannot help you if something goes wrong."

Keira nodded, and held her hands out in front of her, palms facing each other. She breathed — in, then out. In, then out. And a tiny flame was born between her hands. It was a bright little thing, orange and yellow. Keira played with the temperature. First she cooled it to a gentle red, then she heated it and it quickly moved to blue, then white. She kept it small, but it was radiant and so hot she almost dropped it.

Instead, she drew her hands back slowly. They were not burned, it was just her fear playing tricks on her. Keira sweated as she focused on the tiny white flame, then she swept her arm in front of her, stretching it into a thin line of fire. It went from red at one end to white hot at the other and Keira smiled as it hung there.

Secure in her control, Keira sculpted the fire into the shape of a large white horse and sent it galloping around the courtyard. Instead of the clatter of hooves, there was a soft crackle and hiss as steam rose from the ground where it passed. Because she was using magic to fuel the fire, it faded the moment she released her hold on it.

Since there was already steam in the air, Keira moved on to her next experiment without waiting for Declan to prompt her. She condensed the steam slightly at the same time as she produced a bright globe light a few feet away, making a double rainbow appear. Happy with the results, Keira froze the steam and produced several smaller globe lights to dance around them. The light filtered through the crystals, painting the dark earth in a dazzling array of colors.

"Wonderful." Declan said as he started to push himself off the ground.

"Wait! Can I try one more thing?"

He settled back on the dirt, looking at her expectantly.

Keira took a deep breath and closed her eyes, sending her senses into the ground. True spring had come late and there were a great many flowers that hadn't bloomed yet. The ingredients were there, however: seeds, some of them sprouted, and water. Her magic could serve in place of the sun.

She knew how a flower grew, but the plants knew better. Keira only needed to lend them strength and speed. It took only a few minutes of intense focus before she was rewarded for her efforts. The garden sprouted around the edges of the courtyard with a pleasant smell of greenery.

Keira grinned, but pressed on. She wanted to see the garden bloom. It took fifteen minutes of quiet concentration, but inch by inch the bushes and stems grew, some of them as tall as she was when standing. Finally, flowers of all sorts grew and unfurled their fresh petals in a conflagration of white, orange, and scarlet. The heavy floral scent that wafted through the courtyard called to mind the impending summer.

Keira had been focused on her project, but when she looked up she found Declan staring at her. He didn't look pleased, as she had hoped. Rather, he sat ramrod straight, his lips thin and the skin around his eyes tight. He looked....*horrified*.

Keira frowned in confusion. "What's wrong?" She asked.

"You just did something that no one believed possible."

Silence settled between them ,and Declan stared at her for another minute, not bothering to hide his feelings.

"Do you think I could save a poor harvest?" She finally asked. "I could probably do a lot of good with this."

"Aren't you exhausted?" Declan asked, his voice even softer than usual.

"No. Should I be?"

He snorted. "Are you sure you're human?"

Keira glared, but then the dizziness came. She was cold. Colder than she had ever been, although it was more than physical. Her vision shifted and she could swear the air and ground were filled with little threads, tiny connections through which magic flowed. It felt so strange, but she was sure they were real.

He just shook his head. "We're done for the day."

"Good. I think I *am* tired." She laid down right there on the packed dirt.

Declan closed his eyes for a moment and leaned against their tree. "Rest then."

Keira nodded, her external awareness fading as she closed her eyes, finally returned to their usual green.

It was dark when she opened them. She was in her own bed, fully clothed, but tucked under the patchwork quilt she had inherited from her maternal grandmother. Keira was exhausted, her eyes crusty and her mouth dry. She disentangled herself and found the water pitcher. Her hands shook a little as she poured herself a glass, but her legs were perfectly steady.

Her dress clung to her wet body. She could tell it was sweat, but it almost seemed like she had been swimming. She poured a second glass of water, trying to order her thoughts, and spread out her awareness. She wondered what time of day it was. *Where is Declan?*

Her senses found him lying peacefully in his bed. Keira had a third glass of water, then went into her water closet to wash and slip into her nightgown. She wasn't just thirsty, she was famished. She redid her braid and wrapped up in a thick robe, she poked her nose out the door. She was perfectly presentable, if a bit informal.

Keira made her quiet way to the kitchens, her feet cold even in her shoes. The shadows in the hall moved oddly as rain pattered against the exterior windows. When she reached the kitchens, she knocked on the door and was greeted by a yawning cook.

"Sorry to disturb you ma'am. I was just hoping for a snack. I missed dinner."

She nodded pleasantly. "Come in my dear. Have a seat and I'll put on some tea for us."

Keira sat in the chair offered as the plump older woman bustled around the kitchen. She folded her hands on the little kitchen table. "I wasn't sure if anyone would be here this late."

"Oh, someone always works nights in case one of the nobles gets peckish. Their lot don't like waiting."

"Well, I'm lucky then, aren't I." She smiled warmly, "My name is Keira Smith."

"Carolyn Baker." The woman nodded as she put a little pot of something on the table.

"Thank you for taking the time."

"It's no trouble dearie. The night shift gets a bit quiet. I'm glad of the company."

She bustled off and returned a few minutes later with a tea tray. It was a bit extravagant. Keira noticed the little slices of bread were soft and white, and there was imported fruit from the southern isles. She took a slice of orange and chewed it slowly, delighting in the sweetness of it.

"I don't think I've ever had an orange this sweet," she gushed, spreading one of the soft slices of bread with white cheese.

"They just came in from the south, but there's plenty. Don't be shy." Carolyn poured her a steaming mug of golden brown tea. "If you don't mind my asking, why did you miss dinner?"

"I fell asleep after my lessons this afternoon. I don't even remember getting back to my room. Somebody might have carried me."

"Lessons? Are you an academic then?"

Keira hesitated, warming her fingers against the sides of the ceramic mug. "I'm studying magic."

Carolyn went quiet for a moment. "I have a daughter that chose that life."

"Really?"

"Yes, she lives in Polaris, up north. Poor thing does nothing but read. It seems to make her happy though. I get a letter every so often."

"I'm glad she's happy."

Carolyn shrugged. "Is magic that tiring?"

"Apparently." Keira grinned, "It sure took me by surprise."

"Well, you'll know better for next time."

Keira nodded. "I need to talk to my master though. I don't really know why I was so tired."

"Well, that's easy dear. All that energy has to come from somewhere! Seren was always passing out when she first started learning. I could have sworn she slept through every other day — nearly gave me a heart attack more than once. It takes a while to learn your limits." Carolyn patted Keira's hand warmly.

"That makes sense, I suppose." Keira took a sip of the tea and swallowed her thoughts. *Carolyn's daughter must be truly reckless.* From what she understood from Declan and Selene, passing out while attempting magic was *not* a common problem.

"What did you try to accomplish, if I may be so bold?"

"Oh, my master and I were experimenting to see what I might have a knack for. I..." Keira thought back. "I made some fog, manipulated fire, made a rainbow, and then...I grew some flowers." Keira bit her lip.

Carolyn was gaping at her. "All that? Are you sure you weren't dreaming child?"

Keira shook her head. "I'm a Natural. It didn't seem like that much until the flowers."

"I'm surprised this plant growing thing didn't finish you."

Keira shrugged. "My magic took the place of the sun, they didn't need that much."

"And what did you use for the fire?"

"What do you mean?"

"Fuel, girl. What did you fuel the fire with?"

"Also magic..."

"Otherwise known as *yourself*. Dangerous business. You should be more careful."

"I will be. I guess I didn't think about how much energy a plant takes to grow."

"Have another piece of bread." Carolyn said with a soft huff that reminded Keira of her late grandmother.

Keira nodded and took another piece of the barley loaf with a solemness the moment didn't warrant. "Thank you."

* * *

A few days later, Keira sat on the couch in Declan's office with a medical text open in her lap. She had reread the same paragraph at least three or four times. She just wasn't absorbing it. She sighed, flopping against the couch with her eyes on the ceiling. Her brain felt like a sodden sponge from all the studying she had done that day.

She looked over and found Fionn staring at her from the opposite end of the couch. He mouthed what looked like 'beautiful' to himself, but that couldn't be right. Keira looked back down at the book in her lap, heat creeping up her face.

"You've been at it a while, huh?" Fionn laid aside the book he was reading. It was a travel log of Charles the Wanderer, a famous ArKen of their grandparents' generation. Fionn had been reading a lot of ArKen biographies recently.

"What time is it?" Keira closed her book with a snap of finality.

"Break time."

"No, seriously." Keira grinned despite herself, and arched her back in an almost painful, but incredibly satisfying stretch.

"I think it's getting close to tea time."

"Where'd Declan go?" Keira's eyes roved the office.

"He's with a patient."

Keira blinked, "Did he ask me to join him?"

"No — you're fine." Fionn stood and offered her a hand.

"This is too much sitting for one afternoon. Care to join me for a walk?"

The hand that enclosed hers was as warm as she remembered, and it did something strange to her stomach. *No. I can't fall for a noble. For anyone, really. But especially not Fionn.* The fear of getting hurt threatened to saw her heart in half. Keira did her best to hide her reaction, but Fionn gave her an odd look as he pulled her to her feet. He led the way from the room without commenting on it and Keira followed him in silence, hurrying to set her heavy leather-bound book on the edge of Declan's immaculate desk.

Before she knew it, she had followed Fionn all the way to the stables. Entering the soothing darkness helped calm her nerves. She breathed in the familiar smells of horses and clean straw as Fionn touched her elbow to lead her down one of the aisles.

"You haven't met Hurricane yet, have you?"

He had named the mount he purchased that autumn after the terrible storms the Southern Isles sometimes experienced. Personally, Keira thought a horse deserved a sweet name, but when Fionn stopped in front of the animal's stall, she understood. Hurricane's black hair gleamed in the light from the nearest window and his eyes glittered. He was massive, at least fifteen hands high, if not sixteen. He was powerfully built, and she couldn't help but imagine how riding him must feel like riding a thunderstorm. Fionn had known what he was doing when he chose the name.

Despite the intimidation she felt at being near so large a beast, she offered the horse her palm. His velvet lips tickled her as he snuffled over the stall door, snorting and turning to lip at Fionn as he set a hand on the horse's face.

"He's beautiful." Keira breathed.

"And what do you make of his sister?" Fionn tilted his head to indicate the next stall.

Keira approached the door and peeked over to find a white mare chomping her hay. Her coat was a pearlescent white, nearly glowing, with a reddish mane. Her coat looked unreal and Keira couldn't find her voice.

"I bred them myself. But she came out a bit smaller than the rest of their line."

Keira glanced over at Hurricane. He was a giant, but the mare was large too, well over fourteen hands. The mare approached the door, evidently curious about her new visitor.

"Well?" Fionn prompted.

Keira let the horse smell her before stroking its cheek. *How can she be so shiny? So soft? Someone must have brushed her for hours.* "She's beautiful."

"Like her mistress." Fionn said, heat rising in his cheeks as he looked away from Keira, focusing on the horse instead.

Keira's heart sank and she admonished herself again for cherishing feelings she had no right to.

"She's yours."

"What?" She stumbled away from the shining horse to face Fionn.

"She's a gift. You've been riding your parents' mule all this time, right? You need a horse of your own."

"Oh...Fionn." Keira's eyes stung. "I can't accept such an extrav-"

"Runt."

"Excuse me?"

Fionn leaned closer. "She isn't extravagant, I've already told you that she's undersized. I can't sell her. She'd damage my business."

"I can't keep a horse though. I..." Keria bit her lip.

"Why not?"

"Because I...well, she..." It wasn't as though she didn't have the coin to feed her, with her apprenticeship.

Fionn grinned. "She's yours. Deal with it." He bumped his shoulder into hers, gently.

Drat. Why is this man so warm? Keira thought as tingles traveled down her spine.

His face took on a serious look, hazel-brown eyes reflecting the shimmering white horse behind her as he looked down. "If you really don't want her, you don't have to keep her. I may have...overstepped."

Keira set her hand on the side of his tense shoulder and it softened under her touch. She barely recognized her own voice when she found it. "I love her. Thank you, Fionn."

"Would you like to ride her?"

Unable to resist, Keira was in the saddle less than five minutes later. Fionn led the way on Hurricane, and Keira followed. Without planning it, Keira extended her senses in the same way that she did during her morning archery sessions. She could feel the mare in a way she had never done before, so that despite the stiffness of her new leather saddle — another gift from Fionn — she could feel every minuscule movement of her beautiful mount's muscles.

What's more, she could feel the mare's mind. She was so *different* from Cinnamon. The old mule was familiar, warm, and a bit dull. Her new courser was intelligent, not in the way a human was, but much more than Keira knew to expect from a horse. And she was happy to be chasing Hurricane through an open field, with a rider so gentle and responsive. While the mare felt no special fondness for Keira, and they lacked the deep trust that Keira shared with the mule she had grown up riding, her joy was contagious.

She laughed as the wind undid her braid and leaned over her neck. Fionn was faster, of course. Hurricane thundered through the grass at speeds Keira couldn't remember seeing in a horse. But if it was a race, it was one she didn't mind losing. The cobwebs of a day spent buried in books seemed to fall away as they rode, grinning like a pair of idiots until they galloped through a field of wildflowers with the sun warming their backs. They stopped when they reached a stream.

"Fionn, she's the most wonderful gift I've ever received."

Keira gushed as she slid to the soft grass, pulling her skirt after her with an embarrassed flush.

"Do you know what you'll name her?" He asked, jumping to the ground, his eyes averted in the way of a true gentleman.

"Foraminifera. I like her red mane. I'll call her Mini for short."

"Mini suits her." Fionn wore a crooked smile. "I don't think I've ever seen someone so in sync with their mount."

"Oh...thank you." Keira grinned. "But I have an unfair advantage."

His eyebrows knit together in puzzlement.

"I can 'see', without seeing. How do I explain?"

"You mean with your magic?"

Keira nodded. "It's not like I'm making her do anything, but she likes me well enough so she didn't mind working together."

"That makes sense." Fionn took hold of Hurricane's reins and started walking.

"I'm not unsettling you?" She grabbed her own mount's reins.

"No. Why?"

"Communicating with animals isn't really a standard ArKen ability."

"I already knew about it. Besides, why should anything be standard with magic." Fionn shrugged. "Anyone powerful enough to do what I've seen you do is bound to have unique gifts. Plus... Declan had some interesting things to say about your magic the other day."

Keira groaned, but kept pace with him. After a pause, she sighed. "You're unusually comfortable with magic users."

Fionn shrugged, "I've been friends with Declan since we were little kids. Plus, I have a cousin. We're not particularly close, but I was used to being around ArKen long before most people ever meet their first."

"If they do." Keira added.

"If they do." He agreed. "And even though I never progressed as far as *using* magic, I learned a lot about it before I changed courses."

"Want to see something neat?" She asked suddenly.

"As a general rule."

"Keep quiet." She closed her eyes for a moment, pulling some dried apple slices from her pocket.

Within moments Keira became a perch for several songbirds. They mobbed her for the fruit she offered. Her new horse gave an affronted snort, but after the birds took off Keira offered her a whole fresh apple. Mini munched it contentedly.

"How did you do that?"

"The same way I've been talking to her." Keira patted the mare on the side.

"But a domestic horse is one thing. How did you get wild birds to come?"

"It wasn't hard. I can't lie to something that way....or, I don't think I can. So they knew I wouldn't hurt them and that they'd get a sweet meal."

"Dragonsbreath!" He swore.

"It's not that unusual." She couldn't help the pout that pulled at her lips.

"No, it's not that. I was just wondering if you could calm a panicking horse. It could be life or death in an emergency."

"I probably could." Keira smiled widely. *I hadn't thought of that.*

Twelve

When they returned to the castle, Keira headed for her rooms to freshen up before dinner and found her mother waiting in the corridor. Seeing her with her foot tapping and her arms folded, Keira felt herself a child all over again. She'd seen that look many times as a girl.

"Keira Maeve Smith, you have explaining to do." Her mom said in her 'I'm-not-angry-I'm-just-disappointed' voice.

Keira hunched her shoulders as she unlocked her apartment. *What did I do?* She trudged into her rooms with her mom on her heels.

"What were you *thinking*?"

"I have no idea what you're talking about." She said honestly and marched through the rooms to her bedchamber. It didn't matter if her mother saw her underthings.

"You went riding — *alone* — With. A. Man."

"I..." Keira had no defense. *Except that we didn't do anything wrong.*

Her mom threw up her hands and her voice rose for the first time. "Did you think nothing of your reputation!"

"My reputation?" Keira laughed and turned with her dress

half removed, arms caught in the sleeves. "*Seriously?* Why does my reputation matter? We both know I'm never going to marry."

Her mom gasped and answered in a breathy voice, "We know nothing of the sort!"

Keira huffed in disbelief. "Mom, if my being an apprentice ArKen wasn't enough, I took the king's coin. My apprenticeship will take years to complete, and then King Herbert can send me anywhere at a moment's notice, for any reason, for seven more years after that."

"But Keira-"

"No Mom. It isn't what I wanted, but it's a choice I made. I gave up on my prospects. My reputation no longer matters."

"It matters more than ever!" Her mother's voice rose again, her normally dulcet tones coming out harsh. "You're practically a noble!"

Keira's chest tightened painfully, her eyes stinging as she tossed her dress aside and grabbed another. She slipped it over her head to hide her tears. "*'Practically'* is not the same thing as being one. The nobility will hire me, they might even befriend me, but there's no way a noble could ever marry me."

A gentle hand touched her arm and then helped her into her clean dress. Her mom's voice was soft again. "Honey."

She shook her head, Fionn's face rising in her thoughts unbidden. "Even if he wanted to. What duke — or even a baron — would want a smith's daughter in their family line?"

A knock came at the front door.

"I'll get it."

Her mom returned a moment later with a scroll of parchment in her hand, her eyes wide. "You've been invited to dine with Duchess Duval."

"*What!?*" Keira's heart dropped into her stomach.

Her mother pushed her onto the corner of the bed and started plaiting her hair with swift and practiced hands. "Hush. Be polite. You've done nothing wrong and nothing to be ashamed of. Correct?"

Keira turned around and gaped at her mother in open-mouthed disbelief. "*Mother!* Of course we haven't!"

Instead of looking abashed, her mom broke into a giggle. "I was young once." She tutted and turned Keira around again to finish her plait.

When she was done, Keira stood and headed for the hall.

"Wear your necklace!" Her mom called after her.

Keira sighed, wringing her hands nervously. She couldn't keep a duchess waiting, but she did as her mother said and hurried to her dresser to retrieve her single pink glass necklace. When she turned around, her mom was staring at her boots.

"You can't wear those. Trade me." She slipped off her shoes, simple green cloth with a few beads sewn to the top, but much finer than Keira's worn boots. And they matched the frilly green dinner dress she was wearing.

"Thanks Mom." Keira kicked off her boots and slipped into the shoes. Her mom's feet were a little larger than hers, but not by much. The shoes fit comfortably enough.

Her mom hugged her tightly. "Don't forget to curtsy. And be polite."

What does she think I'll do, sass a duchess? Keira shuddered, but nodded her agreement before she stepped into the hallway. She didn't trust herself to speak. She was surprised to find Duchess Duval's messenger was waiting in the hall for her.

"I'm to show you the way."

Keira dipped her head and followed the man until she reached a familiar part of the castle. *Of course, the duchess would live near Dymphna.* Her nerves grew as the man announced her, then directed her to enter. She did so, swiping sweaty palms on a skirt that she wished was thinner. *When did it get so hot?*

"Apprentice Smith." Duchess Duval said as she rose to her considerable height, smoothing her velvet skirt with one hand as she gestured imperiously with the other. Her silver-blonde hair was swept up into a graceful bun, her eyes a startling violet-blue. Her face revealed nothing of her current emotions, although the slight creases near her mouth and eyes gave the impression of someone who spent more time cheerful than cross.

Her apartment was the most beautiful room that Keira had ever seen. It was decorated in soft creams and golds. Seeing the numerous furnishings, her wealth was obvious, yet there was nothing tasteless or gaudy about the rooms. Each piece of furniture seemed chosen for comfort and utility rather than display. But they all happened to be valuable and stylish. How the look was achieved, she had no idea.

Keira remembered her manners belatedly and dropped into a too-deep curtsy. When she straightened, the duchess was smiling at her. *She looks like a cat watching a plump mouse*, Keira decided. And she felt like a mouse, trembling and unable to run as it stared into the amber eyes of death. Amber eyes that reminded her of another pair of much warmer eyes... Keira jerked her attention back to her surroundings.

"Sit with me, won't you?"

Keira hurried to take the seat the duchess offered as Fionn's mother removed the covers from two sumptuous meals.

"What did you think of her?" The older woman asked in a neutral tone.

"Pardon?"

"Fionn's gift."

"Oh, Mini." Keira's fingers wrapped tightly around the base of her chair as she reminded herself to breathe. "She's wonderful. Too much, but wonderful."

"You're the first woman to inspire my son to extravagant gifts." The woman's gaze seemed to see straight through her.

She can read minds. She can definitely read minds.

"Did you ask him for a horse?"

Keira blinked in surprise, but of course a duchess would have no reason to mince words. *Not with me, at least.* "No, Your Grace." Her pulse thudded in her ears and throat. *Will she believe me? What if she doesn't?*

"Have you promised him any favors, magical or otherwise?"

"No." Keira shook her head, her voice breaking on the single word.

A long moment of tense silence passed between them. Then, something wonderful happened. The duchess smiled. And it wasn't the smile of a cat; it was the smile of an indulgent mother. "I thought not. My Fionn is no fool."

"He's my...friend." Keira murmured, then sucked her lip. Then she remembered where she was and schooled her features.

"Is that all?" Duchess Duval turned her attention to her plate. "Fionn may find that disappointing."

"What else could he be?" Keira blurted, immediately wishing she could swallow her own words.

"The third son of a noble house and a Natural ArKen of unusual potency?" She raised an eyebrow. "Surely you don't think Fionn gifts all of his friends with horses."

"Well...no." Keira's heart was racing for an entirely new reason.

"I've never known my son to take such an interest in books as he has this last season or two. Perhaps he'll find work as a scholar. I'm sure the two of you will have plenty to discuss."

Keira's hands shook as she speared a bite of herb-roasted chicken, but she couldn't bring it to her mouth. Her eyebrows felt permanently crinkled. "You...you don't object to us...discussing... books?"

"Perhaps a chaperon in future." The Duchess raised one perfectly sculpted eyebrow.

"Yes, Your Grace."

"Your master would serve well enough."

"Thank you, Your Grace."

"A Natural may refer to me simply as 'Duchess'."

Keira's eyes grew as wide as saucers. *I could never.*

Duchess Duval gave a familiar crooked smirk, the resemblance to her son striking in that moment. "Perhaps after you complete your training?"

Keira spent the rest of the meal answering questions about her apprenticeship, and especially about her study sessions and the friends who joined her. The duchess was curious about the oddest things, but like Fionn, showed no discomfort at the amount of power Keira possessed. Instead, she seemed to weigh her answers against some other metric. It was strange, like taking one of Declan's exams, except she had no indication of how she was doing. At long last, what felt like an hour or more after they had finished eating, Duchess Duval stood and led Keira to the door.

"Fionn could do *much* worse." There was amusement in her voice.

Keira whirled, but the door was already shut. She stood in the corridor, confused and exhausted, fighting with the electric feeling that coursed through her. *Is it really okay for me to court Fionn?*

* * *

A few days later, Keira arrived in Declan's office for an afternoon study session and found Fionn already there, playing with a puzzle box. He looked up and greeted her as she sat down, but Declan didn't seem to notice her arrival. Bright sunshine streamed in from the window, yet a tense silence filled the room. Declan's eyes were trained on an official-looking missive on his desk. His thinking-wrinkle was firmly in place, carved deeper than she had yet seen.

She leaned in to whisper to Fionn. "What's going on?"

Declan answered without looking up, his voice giving nothing away, "We need to have a serious conversation. Fionn, you should make yourself scarce."

As Declan spoke, Fionn straightened in his seat and set his puzzle box aside. He set his hands on the arms of his chair to rise, but without conscious thought, Keira's hand shot out to rest on Fionn's forearm, holding him in place.

Declan met her eyes and shrugged. "This is a personal letter from King Herbert. All ArKen living in the castle are to compose a brief summary of their abilities and submit them to the chancellor's office. The king has closed the border with Eimar. We are advised to prepare ourselves for war."

Keira stared at Declan for a moment, horror rising in her chest and an odd rushing sound in her ears.

"I know that this is unexpected."

Keira shook her head. "Not really. The castle smiths have been working on nothing but orders for the guard the last few weeks, mostly arrowheads."

"It's never a good sign when the western border closes." Fionn agreed, his hand closing around her numb fingers.

Keira swallowed, grateful for the warmth. "I have to compose a 'summary'?"

"As your master, that duty falls to me." Declan licked his lips. "It will be a complicated report, given your potential."

Fionn's hand tightened around hers. "Do you think she'll be sent to the front lines?"

"We don't know that there will *be* front lines," he hedged.

"*Declan.*" Fionn's voice held a dangerous note Keira had never heard there before.

He gave a heavy sigh. "It's possible."

Keira felt like ice was spiraling out from her belly. It took everything she had to control her breathing.

"I will advise that, should we be needed, you be allowed to serve with the healers or that the king utilize your ability to communicate with animals. But, King Herbert may choose to ignore my suggestions."

"Her training isn't finished." Fionn pointed out.

"And I'll emphasize that." Declan agreed.

Was the room always spinning? Keira was surprised when she felt a warm pair of tears drip down her face. She wiped them away and took a deep breath through her nose, then another. "It isn't time to worry yet, right?"

She barely heard their reassurances. War was coming; the kingdom had been abuzz with the expectation for months. And it was enough to make Keira wish she was still trying to snuff out her magic, *hang the consequences.* She wrapped her free hand around her middle, aware she was slouching but unable to do anything about it. *Why did I have to take the king's coin? Stupid. Stupid. Stupid.*

Fionn gave her hand a tight squeeze and she came back to the present.

"They might not call in the ArKen at all."

Keira nodded. Unfortunately, she knew the smells of blood and burning flesh all too well from her work in Declan's clinic, and she couldn't get them out of her mind. At least in the clinic, she could soothe herself with the knowledge she was helping people. War might break her.

* * *

*Keira floated in the dark, too weak to move. She gasped for breath, and her lungs were strangely hot. She struggled against the weight on her chest until she felt like her limbs were burning with invisible fire. She couldn't cry out because she was too weak, but she wept silently. Taking shallow breaths, she finally managed to wrench herself out of the dark water.....*and rolled onto her bedroom floor with a solid thump.

She lay there gasping. Keira looked around wildly with silver eyes, half blind with the mists of her dream clinging to her consciousness. She was drenched in sweat, and as soon as she understood where she was, Keira crawled over to the water pitcher. It was nearly empty, but she poured herself half a glass of water and gulped it down. She moved to the couch and sat there for a while, rubbing her hip where she'd fallen on it.

Keira wondered what time it was. After a brief and failed attempt at going back to sleep, she decided to get dressed for the day. She slid into her magically heated bath with a sigh of relief as her aching muscles loosened. But she cut her bath short. Keira wanted to be moving. She pulled her long hair into a neat braid as quickly as she could and stuck a small butterfly pin in the side, then went for a walk. She needed to clear her mind.

She followed some instinct that drew her to high ground. Keira felt a little shaky as she climbed the endless flights of stairs and emerged on the battlements. She didn't even know if she was allowed up here, but she breathed in the gray air of the early dawn with a sigh of relief.

Keira walked forward and found a clear space with a table and a couple of chairs. She sat and stared out over the dark stone of the crenelated battlements and across the castle grounds. It was too dark to see much, other than a handful of lanterns as servants began their work for the day. Everything was silent.

"Couldn't sleep?" A young guard asked her, leaning against the half wall that formed the edge of the roof.

She shook her head. "Am I in the way?" She asked quietly.

"I'm not on duty. I couldn't sleep either."

She noticed the silver band on his sleeve that marked him as a battlemage just as Declan and Selene joined them.

"Trouble sleeping?" She asked them.

"Nightmare." Selene said simply.

"You too?" Declan quirked an eyebrow.

They all stood or sat quietly for a half hour, collecting themselves. But they weren't alone. Before long, there were roughly a dozen ArKen gathered on the roof. Everyone looked shaken, but the calm of the early dawn soon soothed their frayed nerves. Nobody seemed inclined to explain why they were on the roof.

"Did we all have the same dream?" Selene finally asked.

"It was dark," Keira said. "I was helpless."

"And in pain," Declan agreed with a nod. "I couldn't breathe."

"There was fire," the young guard added, "Or maybe it was just pain. It felt like being burned."

"It did." Keira agreed.

"What does it mean?" A little girl that she didn't recognize asked.

"It means some great magic has been worked, and not something good," Declan said, his thinking-wrinkle prominent as he leaned on the stone crenelation at the edge of the roof.

The guards among them nodded and one of them asked, "But who would have the power?"

"A group?" Keira asked, "But what kind of magic was it?"

"I believe a magical illness has been unleashed." Declan said with a frown.

"It floats on the wind, but it isn't coming here." Selene said firmly.

"Where then?" The little girl asked, shivering in her nightgown.

Selene wrapped her shawl around the young Natural. *At least I think she's a Natural. She's too young to have started training otherwise.*

Selene tilted her head, her gaze distant. "North. But I can't tell any more than that."

"That's more than the rest of us." Declan said seriously.

"No wonder His Majesty urged us to prepare for war," one of the battlemages added.

Keira's stomach swooped unpleasantly at the reminder. "We have to tell the king." She concluded, springing to her feet.

The battlemages nodded.

The youngest of the guards said, "We'll approach the chancellor right away. I think we should all go. This is no small matter."

Keira shivered, but it wasn't from the cold.

* * *

King Herbert received their group within a half hour. Keira noticed that he looked distinctly disheveled and wondered if he'd been roused early. She also noted that the magical members of the royal guard subtly placed themselves between the other ArKen and the king. Declan was the only outside ArKen whom they seemed to regard as perfectly trustworthy.

King Herbert settled himself in his padded throne with an almost-suppressed groan. The deep purple of the upholstery was the only real color in the throne room, not that it lacked comfort. A massive fireplace sat unlit at the opposite end of the room, and several bearskin rugs overlapped to block the chill of the dark flagstone beneath their feet. Keira's eyes were drawn to the walls, where every inch was covered with tapestries woven in rich and varied shades of brown.

Despite the intricate beauty of the tapestries, Keira's attention soon returned to the king. She had never been in the same room as royalty before. Keira bit her lip and pretended that she didn't notice the king massaging his knee. One glance at her master told her Declan had noticed as well.

"Why have you requested an audience? I understand there has been something of an uproar among the ArKen of the castle."

The group curtsied and bowed, then looked amongst themselves until someone stepped forward.

"Your Majesty," the young battlemage said in a voice laced with respect that bordered on reverence, "We all experienced a shared dream early this morning."

The king frowned, but straightened in his throne and motioned for the man to continue.

"It was a nightmare. After discussing it amongst ourselves we believe that there is an illness-"

"You're ill?" King Herbert asked, visibly alarmed.

"No, Your Majesty. I'm not explaining well."

Selene stepped forward. "Your Majesty, we believe that some impossibly strong ArKen or group of ArKen has unleashed an illness up north. We can only guess at the target, but something terrible is coming."

"An illness? And you believe it is of a *magical* nature?" The king cleared his throat and took a slow breath. In that momentary pause, any trace of anxiety was wiped from his face. "Will ordinary medicine be effective in treating the victims?"

How does he manage to look so regal with his clothes rumpled?

"I doubt it, Sire." Declan replied, "And it feels airborne. If it proves contagious, it could spread like a plague."

"Your Majesty?" Keira heard herself speak, and quickly curtsied deeply, shocked at her own boldness.

"Yes, Mistress...?"

"Apprentice Smith. I don't think it is an ordinary illness. I suspect that it will primarily target ArKen. I'm almost certain of it." She was pleased that her voice remained steady, even if her legs trembled. But she couldn't have explained herself. It was just that the fire in her dream seemed to burn away at her magic, her very life essence.

"Does everyone share this belief?"

"No, Sire. There's no way for us to know that," one of the older battlemages said.

Declan bowed low. "Your Majesty, I am training Apprentice Smith, and I believe that we should trust her intuition. She has a uniquely powerful gift."

"She's our new Natural?" The king eyed her with renewed interest.

"Yes, Sire. But I believe her gift is powerful, even among that elite group. We should trust her instincts."

"Apprentice Smith, what makes you believe that this illness will target ArKen?" He addressed her directly, shifting on his throne.

"In the dream, it felt like my magic was on fire."

"That's all?"

She nodded fervently. "Yes Sire."

He looked at Declan. "Master Elers, that doesn't sound...." When Declan nodded, King Herbert continued, "But if this is an illness aimed at ArKen, what can be done?"

"It would tell us the likely target." One of the guards in the room, not part of their group, spoke up.

"Polaris." Several people, including King Herbert, chorused.

"But how do we help them? Is there anything that can be done?"

"Keira can ask a few fast birds to carry notes to the University." Declan said.

Keira shook her head as the heavy weight of responsibility dropped onto her shoulders. "They won't understand. I can ask them to fly north, but not specifically to Polaris. I might have a little more luck if I'm looking at a map, but geography isn't my strong suit." She felt tears sting her eyes and held them back with difficulty.

King Herbert pointed at one of the guards." Bring this woman a map, immediately. "And something to write with. Do your best, Apprentice Smith. No one can ask for more, even your king."

She dropped a swift curtsy. "I will do what I can, Sire. Thank you."

"If we send a party of healers to Polaris will they just get ill?" King Herbert asked Declan.

"There's really no way to know, but I think we must risk it. If this is an attack on your ArKen, then someone is planning something big."

"Wiping out our ArKen would be a massive advantage if King Duncan is planning an invasion." King Herbert said thoughtfully.

Selene stepped forward, her hands on the youngest ArKen's shoulders. The little girl looked at them with wide eyes as Selene spoke, "Your Majesty, perhaps we should send the children to their beds?"

The king nodded, and the young Natural was sent away, along with an apprentice Keira guessed was eleven or twelve. He looked like he wanted to argue, but didn't dare — not when the king had spoken.

"Weakening our ArKen is an advantage Eimar would certainly

need for a war to turn in their favor." King Herbert said as the door closed behind the youngsters. "Very well, I will send a party north toward Polaris. But it must be voluntary. I will not order anyone to travel to a place where we know they will be in grave danger. And we cannot send all of our ArKen away, if this is somehow a ruse to leave the capital vulnerable."

"I would be happy to lend my services as healer, Your Majesty." Declan said.

Keira stepped up beside him. "I go where my teacher goes, with your blessing."

King Herbert smiled warmly. "You are brave. The both of you."

"I'm willing to go as well, Your Majesty, though I can't guarantee I'll be much help."

"Thank you, Mistress Morgan."

Nobody else volunteered for a few minutes, but eventually the young battlemage stepped forward. "I'll go too, Sire. I'm no healer, but I can make sure they get there in one piece."

King Herbert stood. "Thank you to those who have volunteered. You will be accompanied by a few guards, but I think it would be unwise to send more of the limited ArKen we have." He addressed Declan directly, "I will make the arrangements and you should be able to leave by noon, unless you need to make your own preparations?"

Declan shook his head. "We will be ready by noon, Sire. Thank you," he finished with a tight bow.

The King left the room to the bows and curtsies of all present.

When the writing supplies arrived, Selene penned the letter. Her penmanship was tidiest, and she was able to produce four copies at once. While she worked, Keira studied the map, paying careful attention to the sorts of landmarks she thought would hold any meaning for a bird.

Declan led her onto the roof, and waited patiently while she looked for something to help. She found three swifts and a peregrine, but she was unsure if they understood her. One of the swifts seemed to like the idea of a long journey, but she had little confidence that he would continue if he got hungry or lost interest. The peregrine understood her a little better, and she was able to impress on him that she had a journey to make as well, but if he returned to her after they were both done, he would always have food. He liked the bargain.

Thirteen

After her dubious letter-sending, Keira practically ran to her rooms. She grabbed her bag and threw her handful of dresses into it. After brief consideration, she left the fancy pink dress in her wardrobe, but rolled up her hooded cloak and shoved it in the bag. She threw several sets of underthings and stockings into the bag. All she had clean. Her dagger also went into the bag, along with some soap and a comb. She pulled her decorative hairpin out and left it on her dresser.

It could take as long as a week to reach Polaris, so Keira pulled the lightest blanket off her bed and laid it between the handles of her canvas bag. She glanced longingly at the book her Aunt had given her when she was young, but decided against it. Instead she lifted her bow and quiver off the wall and slung them across her back. She grabbed her bag and ran to her father's forge to tell him that she would be absent.

When he saw her face, he dropped his hammer. "What's going on?"

She didn't dare tell him what was going on, not in front of the other smiths. They hadn't been expressly forbidden by the king, but it seemed the sort of thing that shouldn't be shared.

"I'm traveling to Polaris as part of my duty to the king. Something has happened, and they need healers." That was as much as she dared share. Nobody had thought to swear the ArKen to secrecy, but she knew it was best, especially with the other smiths standing there. *Gossiping magpies, the lot of them,* she thought fondly.

"Dragonsbreath!" He swore loudly enough for several other smiths to glance over. He held up the arrowhead he was working on meaningfully. "I don't want you traveling right now."

"I've promised the King, Pa. And I believe I can help. I have to go."

"Then I'm coming with you." He wiped his hands on his apron.

"No. There's nothing you can do. Besides, His Majesty is providing an escort of guards."

He fought with himself a moment, then sighed. "Be careful."

"I will."

"Promise me." He grabbed her shoulders.

"I promise you, Pa. I'll be careful." She hugged him tightly.

Little more than an hour had passed by the time Keira dropped her bag outside Mini's stall. It wouldn't bother her horse, and Keira needed to find the rest of the party. It proved an easy task, since she had the benefit of her magical perception. Declan was in his office, talking with another healer and packing medicine. With only a brief detour to hug her mother goodbye, Keira hurried to join him.

"We'll need something for fever." Keira said, looking over his shoulder. He seemed to be focused on their breathing.

Declan pointed at a cabinet and Keira went to gather the dried herbs hanging there. Declan was pale and sweaty as he moved fretfully around his office.

"I think that's everything." He finally said.

"What about a change of clothes?" Keira asked, "And a cloak."

He almost slapped his forehead. "Of course!"

Keira slung the three full bags of medicine across herself. "I'll get these to the stables. You go pack yourself and meet me there."

He nodded, then paused. "You didn't have to come."

"If I wanted to avoid sick people, I've chosen an odd specialty."

Declan smiled down at her.

There seemed to be a lot to do. Despite the fact that Keira thought she was ready to go within an hour of speaking to the king, she and the other ArKen wound up running all over the castle fetching supplies for the journey. It would take at least five days to ride to Polaris. It was two hundred miles to Polaris, and the forest would slow them down considerably.

Dymphna, of all people, saddled Mini and then led Hurricane to stand beside her.

"I don't think Fionn's coming," Keira said.

"No, he ordered his horse." Dymphna shrugged. "It might have nothing to do with your group, but he ordered feed for him too."

Dymphna bit her lip, still holding Hurricane's lead. "Keira...I know I'm not the most comfortable around ArKen in general... but...please be careful."

Keira embraced her. "I will. Thank you. I know you've been trying."

As if she could understand, Mini nosed Dymphna's hand.

Dymphna grasped her forearm. "Are you sure about this? I mean...a few months ago you didn't have any magic and now... this is a big deal."

"I always had magic. I just wasn't using it."

She shrugged, "Same thing."

"I have to go help."

Her friend nodded. "I get it. I'll just worry about you. Arielle too. She'll be mad she missed seeing you off."

Keira gave her friend one final squeeze as Fionn quickly stuffed his saddlebags and claimed Hurricane's reins.

"You're coming?" Declan called across the courtyard.

"Of course I am." Fionn called back in his deep voice, eyes jumping to Keira in a way that made her heart race.

Declan frowned, his worry-line making an appearance. "Why? You won't be any good. We're going to fight a plague."

"An extra pair of hands is always useful, besides, traveling with a noble has perks."

"I *am* a noble." Declan pointed out.

"Barely."

"Ouch." Declan slapped a hand to his heart.

Fionn chuckled. "You know what I mean."

He shrugged. "This will be hazardous, to say the least."

"I know. That's why I can't wait around here while you and your beautiful young apprentice traipse halfway across the kingdom."

"Gee, and here I thought you were coming for my benefit." Declan replied, his voice dripping with sarcasm.

Keira ducked to hide her face. *How can Fionn say something like that where anyone could hear.* She put cooling hands to her flushed cheeks as the party prepared to embark. Arielle arrived at the last moment, breathless, to hug her goodbye. Keira was overwhelmed by hugs and presents.

Arielle shivered, her bright yellow dress brilliant against her tawny skin, and passed her a pack of cookies and a bag of apples. "Watch out for wolves."

"Wolves won't be an issue for our Keira." Declan said confidently.

"I don't know. There probably isn't a lot I can do when an animal is hungry."

"Just come back safe, okay? You too Declan." Arielle blushed prettily and handed him a matching package. "I brought you some cookies as well."

He bent to kiss her cheek then swept up into the saddle. "Be well while we're away."

Keira saw Arielle slip a book into Declan's saddlebag, her face bright red from the kiss.

The group of ArKen set off at a walking pace, their nervous energy making the horses move faster. Four ArKen, one stubborn noble, and half a dozen guards cantered down the road for almost two hours before Keira pulled Mini back to a slower pace.

"We'll wear the horses out. They have to continue all day." She called to Declan.

He nodded and held his arm up in a sign for the group to slow down.

"Can we walk for a few minutes, actually?" Selene asked sheepishly, "I'm not really used to the saddle."

"If you can make it another twenty minutes there's a stream where we can water the horses." The battlemage said.

"I can. Thank you…what was your name?"

"Liam, ma'am."

"That's my father's name." Keira said automatically.

"It's pretty common." He replied, shrugging.

Keira blushed a little, feeling her old shyness creep over her, but Fionn pulled alongside and made some joke she barely heard. She laughed, feeling a bit better just by his presence. *How did he know I needed rescuing?* She smiled warmly at him, then blushed anew remembering that he had publicly called her beautiful.

"Can you sense the stream?" Fionn asked her.

"Don't be ridiculous." Selene said. "How would she do that?"

He shrugged. "Fish have brains, surely."

Keira obediently closed her eyes and sent her mind ahead of them. Her senses searched along the ground until she found the stream. It was true, there were quite a few fish, but they were not responsive in the same way birds were. She borrowed a finch's eyes and saw the stream from above. When she opened her eyes, she could see the silver of her irises reflected in Fionn's serious amber eyes.

"We're closer than you thought," she told Liam. "I'd guess just five or ten minutes."

Selene was taken aback. "How did you find it?"

"Well, I did find some fish, but I didn't need them. The

ground and water are teeming with life. I couldn't tell how far it was." Keira hesitated before adding, "I looked through a bird."

"What?" Selene and Liam squawked together.

"It didn't hurt him." Keira said defensively. "He was happy to show off, actually, since I can't fly."

"Let me clarify." Selene said in a tight voice. "How?"

Keira shrugged, "This isn't something I find difficult, so I don't really understand what you're asking."

"Forget sensing the ground and water itself. How did you 'look through' another creature?"

"Extrasensory perception." Keira said confidently. "Declan taught me."

Fionn laughed. "He taught you what to call it. Declan can't do that."

"Is it really that unusual?"

"Yes." A dozen voices answered.

Keira hunched a little. She hadn't realized everyone was listening.

"Hey, cheer up. That's a useful skill." Fionn said quietly.

"It's hard standing out." Selene added knowingly.

Keira was grateful that someone understood. She tried to sit up a little straighter but was suddenly too aware of her limbs. *What do people do with their feet when they're riding? It it normal to rest one hand on your thigh?* She buried it in Mini's russet mane instead.

It didn't take long for the sidelong glances to subside, but Keira decided she was done sharing her magic for a while. Soon, the smell of fresh water and the sound of splashing reached them. The bank was a little steep for the horses, so Fionn and a couple of the guards climbed down and filled buckets for them.

She glanced up at the blue sky. Something felt odd about it.

Selene saw her looking. "Yes, I believe it will rain this afternoon."

"Is that what I'm feeling?"

"Probably." Selene shrugged. "It should just be a little drizzle."

"So you can sense the water and temperatures up there?"

Selene's forehead creased. "I suppose I can. I never really thought about it. I was taught that it wasn't possible."

The next time they stopped to water the horses, Keira stifled a laugh at how Selene was walking. It seemed she was the only one among them who was unused to riding. Keira had to help her rub out a cramp in her thigh, adding a little magical healing when Selene nodded in response to her quizzical raised brow.

"Whose land is this?" One of the guards asked. He held three horses' reins while some of his fellows stepped away to relieve themselves.

"My eldest brother's." Fionn said.

"He won't mind us using his stream?"

Fionn shook his head. "You'd have to be a horse's ass to have that attitude."

The guard shrugged. "He wouldn't be the first noble overprotective of his lands."

Fionn laughed. "True enough."

Keira looked around in amazement. *This is part of the Duvals' holdings?* She couldn't imagine owning land. Looking up, she was surprised to see a peregrine. She reached out to greet her little friend, but it was a different bird and shied away from her mental touch. She didn't press it, instead leaning against Mini.

She started absently braiding her mane while she waited for her turn to use their makeshift privy. She picked up where she left off when she got back, and by the time the group was finally ready to set off again, her horse had several long red braids hanging down her shining white neck. Mini tolerated this treatment admirably and got a carrot for her patience.

By the time they mounted again, it was getting windy. They passed more farmland as the morning waned. The patchwork of green and amber fields was broken up by lines of trees and small streams. Every so often she would see a wise old tree standing alone in a farmer's field.

"Why do they leave a tree in the middle of their fields? It seems like it would be a pain to plant around it?" Keira asked no one in particular.

On either side of her, Selene and Fionn shrugged.

The ArKen guard, Liam, replied, "Some say it's to act as lightning rods. I've heard that it helps make the soil richer, but my dad left a few trees just because he liked them. He always ate lunch in the shade of the nearest one."

Keira pondered that.

"I doubt it's for lightning. If it is, it isn't very efficient. None of these trees are burned." Selene said after a moment.

"You have to admit, they are aesthetically pleasing." Fionn added.

Keira grinned at him. "That they are, and no doubt the shade is a relief on sunny days. Thank you for solving our mystery, Liam." She added, turning to the guard.

They briefly stopped for a late lunch and to stretch their legs, but nobody wanted to pause for long. The wind had turned biting, and it had started to sprinkle. Keira pulled the hood up on her cloak after she mounted Mini.

The afternoon passed slowly in a haze of cold wet and ill humor. Everyone was stressed, and nobody had much to say. Keira was relieved when someone suggested an inn. They pressed a little later than was really comfortable to make it there, but as it was growing truly dark and everyone's stomachs were growling they finally came upon the Silver Lady.

Everyone dismounted. The party of travelers was cold, wet, and stank of horse. Their spirits rose at the thought of a warm fire and full bellies. A couple of hands came to stable their horses. Two of the guards stayed to help since there were so many horses, but everyone else headed into the inn.

* * *

The Silver Lady was surprisingly rustic for its name. Great wooden beams stretched across the ceiling, and the floor was some kind of dark stone. Keira thought it might have been brown, but it was hard to tell because it was covered in soot and dirt. Soot also coated the off-white walls. The largest table was taken, so the group split up and settled at three free tables. Keira sat with Fionn, Selene, and three of the guards. Declan sat at the next table with Liam and four more guards. They were still close enough for conversation, but the five uniformed guards that made up the rest of their party had to sit on the other side of the smoky taproom.

Keira approached the bar with Fionn and Liam. The fire in the hearth glinted on the silver armband of Liam's uniform as he took a stool while they waited for the innkeeper to notice them. It was a few minutes. He was busy with the group at the large table.

Finally, he returned to the bar and approached the three of them, wiping his hands on his stained apron. "How can I help ye gents, little lady?'

"We need dinner and lodging. And perhaps baths."

"I'm sure I can rustle up something for yeh. But for so many, the baths will be cold. And ye'll have to share a room."

"All eleven of us?" Fionn asked in surprise.

"Yes. We're a bit full. I on'y have one room left…anyone ever tell you yer the spitting image of Severin Duval?"

Fionn nodded and dropped a coin purse on the counter. "He's my older brother."

"Well, now…." The man bowed low before continuing, "I'm sure I could find a little more space for your lordship. Did you want yer dinner down here or in yer rooms?"

"Down here is fine. How much will we owe you?"

The innkeeper did some quick math on his hands. "Eleven guests with meals and baths…twenty copper should do."

"Thank you." Keira said sweetly as Fionn counted it out.

He shrugged, and added a silver to the pile. "For your trouble."

The innkeeper bowed, then quickly swept the coins off the counter. "One of the girls will bring ye yer dinner in a moment."

"Will he kick someone else out?" Keira whispered.

"I doubt it. More likely, he saved a room for rich guests, or is giving up his own sleeping quarters." Fionn grimaced. "Normally, I would have made sure, but we *are* traveling on an errand for the king."

Keira nodded, although she felt a twinge of guilt, and followed him back to their table.

The food was delicious, if simple. Even the nobles among them had nothing to complain of. And nobody had to take a cold bath. Between the four ArKen, it wasn't too much trouble to heat the tub several times. Declan was almost useless for the task, but the other three managed it easily. Selene was well practiced with her tea, Liam was a specialized battlemage, and Keira had made a study of heat.

When they finally went to their rooms, Keira was delighted that she and Selene got to share a large featherbed. As it turned out, the innkeeper kept two fancy rooms in reserve in case a noble visited. The party shared those two rooms, two ArKen to each, along with several guards. Keira wouldn't have minded sleeping on the floor, but the gentlemen insisted. As a result, she drifted to sleep on a feather cloud. She was warm, dry, and pleasantly tired from the day's ride.

* * *

Everything was dark and Keira choked on the fire that ran through her veins. She gasped, but her lungs burned too. She struggled weakly against the weight of her limbs, and looking down saw that a vine had attached itself to her legs and was pulsing with an inky darkness. It was killing her!

She sat bolt upright in bed, and looked around wildly. It took a minute to realize where she was, but when she recognized the room at the Silver Lady, a little reason came back to her. She turned to her right and saw Selene had the same wild look. She touched her arm and waited for her companion to focus on her face.

"Did you have the dream too?" Keira whispered hoarsely.

Selene nodded. Her hair was sticking to her neck from the cold sweat of the nightmare, but Keira was sure that she looked no better. She tossed the heavy blanket off of them, relieved that she had the strength. Getting to her feet, she motioned for Selene to follow. One of the guards was a light sleeper and looked up as they were leaving. Selene motioned for him to come as well.

The group of three crept down to the taproom, where they found Declan, Liam, and Fionn gathered around the hearth with fragrant mugs of mulled cider. The young girl who had served them went to fetch more as soon as she saw the new arrivals. Before anyone had said a word, they joined their companions and sat sipping quietly.

"I didn't expect us to repeat the dream," Declan finally said.

"It was different this time," Keira added.

"How so?" Liam quirked an eyebrow.

"The vines. Did you see them last time?"

The guard shook his head.

"Neither did I. Nor this time. Did anyone else see vines?" Declan asked the group at large.

Selene shook her head.

"Did they seem important?" Fionn asked.

"*Very.* I think whatever we're looking for originated in the forest. We should look there, not Polaris."

"Just because you dreamed about some plants, doesn't-" Liam started.

"Keira is uniquely connected to the land," Fionn said firmly.

When Liam scoffed Declan added, "It's true. I saw her grow a flower garden in fifteen minutes."

"Bull." Liam spat.

"And she could find the stream," Selene added thoughtfully.

"Don't be stupid. She told us herself that was because a little birdie told her."

"The difference in her dream may be because she's a Natural," Selene suggested.

Keira took a deep breath, centering herself. She tried to speak up several times, but the others continued to bicker. Finally she had had enough. *QUIET,* she yelled mentally. Every ArKen's eyes turned to her.

"I am certain we will find the source of this illness in the forest. At the very least we can ask around when we pass through Oaklyra. Perhaps they've had other ArKen pass through recently."

Fionn nodded and moved to sit beside her, putting a protective arm around her shoulders. "It wouldn't hurt to ask."

Keira felt herself blush, but hoped it wouldn't show in the low light of the fire. Fionn smelled like leather and soap. His arm was warmer than she would have expected and she narrowly avoided snuggling into him. *Very* narrowly. If they had been alone, she certainly would have. She glanced up and saw he was holding himself a little stiffly, as if he had suddenly realized he was draped across a maiden.

"Excuse me," a mousy voice interrupted.

They all looked over to see their serving girl, holding her empty tray like a shield. She was younger than Keira had realized, perhaps only fourteen, and her arms were trembling.

"What is it, miss?" Liam asked, his mien softening.

"I don' mean to-to interrupt you. Great persons such as yerselves." She curtsied prettily. "I couldn't help but overhear that yer headed to Oaklyra?"

"We are," Declan acknowledged.

Fionn's posture relaxed, though his arm was still draped around Keira. "Please speak freely. We don't bite."

"S-sorry...we're not used to so many mages 'round these parts. I just thought you should know. There've been bandits on the road. Travelers have been comin' out of the forest in rough shape if they come at all."

"It's kind of you to warn us." Selene said with a warm smile.

"So you'll choose a different route?" The girl asked hopefully.

Their previously silent guard shook his head. "We're on the king's orders. It would cost us too much time. The warning is useful though. Thank you, miss."

She received a round of nods and thanks, bobbed a quick curtsy, and left. Keira smiled to herself, knowing she would have felt the same at the girl's age. *More recently than that, if I'm honest with myself.* She took a sip of her cider and relaxed into Fionn's side. The small group continued discussing the matter at hand, but Keira soon felt her eyelids fluttering and drifted off to sleep.

She dreamed about running across a meadow. She was a horse and Mini ran beside her. When she woke up, it was in her bed with Selene. Everyone dressed quickly, the men stepping into the hall to allow the women some privacy. Then they made their way to the taproom for a quick bowl of porridge.

Most of the men carried their bags out and saddled the horses, while Keira, Selene, and the guard who had joined them last night, a man named Marcus, discussed the bandit situation with the innkeeper. He was insistent that it was a smaller problem than their server had made it seem. Lots of guests had come through the forest without issue, but he was able to point out the place where incidents had happened on a map.

They met the rest of their group outside a few minutes later. Keira immediately swung into the saddle, brushing Mini's mind with her own. She was surprised to find the image of herself running as a horse. She didn't know how she felt about sharing a dream with her mount, but it seemed it had made the mare happy. She slipped her half an apple as they set out, holding the other half out to Fionn. Hurricane took it from her hand before his rider had time to react. Both of them laughed as they set out on their gleaming horses.

The lands they passed were incredibly flat. Beets and chard were ripening in the fields, and hay had already been gathered into large wheels on one or two of the farms. They dried in the sun.

The cultivated land soon gave way to wild plains and the party grew quieter. Keira felt exposed and was relieved when they were able to skirt the forest for a while. She noticed the guards eyed the shadows under the trees with suspicion, but she felt safer.

The land opened up again for an hour or two before they finally entered the trees. Keira's pale skin was a little pink from the sun, so she was glad of the shadows. The cool air soothed her skin and the soft dark eased her strained eyes. Picking up on the nervousness of the guards, she let her mind unfurl and flitted from one woodland creature to another, checking for disturbances. They were the only ones around and she told the others so, but it didn't seem to make their guards feel any more at ease.

Fourteen

After a couple hours of quiet riding through the woods, the party arrived at the Patchwork Hearth, an inn at the edge of Oaklyra. The town itself was surprisingly small, considering the fame of their bows. The houses were sturdy and practical, with none of the decorative frills she was expecting. Keira looked around, glad to see the residents seemed perfectly happy to have visitors. Not all small towns were as welcoming; Stoneybrooke certainly wasn't.

The travelers were shown to the stables first, and Keira was relieved to see fresh hay and clean stalls. The boy who stabled the horses was gentle with them, and horses greeted him from other stalls. She listened and saw him as they did, a mixture of soft touches, quiet singing, warm mash, and sugar cubes. Keira grinned.

The Patchwork Hearth was a lovely inn. The interior was clean and open. The taproom was two stories tall and had good ventilation so that it wasn't nearly as smoky as the last inn had been. The walls were nearly untouched by the smoke, and the bright hickory gave the place a cozy appearance. Several long tables sat at one end of the room, while the other side was filled with smaller round tables.

Everything inside was made of different kinds of wood. Keira smiled as she thought that the place was well named. The contrast between the wooden furniture created an odd patchwork that was surprisingly warm and appealing. And the chairs were upholstered with matching green quilted material that seemed to pull the place together.

A bard played a half harp near the large, open hearth. He seemed skilled, though Keira knew she wasn't likely to know the difference. She and a few others approached the bar while the rest of the group claimed one of the long wooden tables. She tapped her foot on the hardwood floor in time to the rambunctious music. The bard had a nice voice — deep, but not so deep that it was hard to hear.

Keira indulged in a melomel mead to go with her dinner of sausages and squash. It was perhaps a little stronger than she realized, and she soon felt bolder than she normally would. As the bard continued to play, she dragged Fionn to his feet to dance. There were several couples dancing, but it was a much wilder dance than those Fionn would be used to. He smiled the whole time and held her closer than strictly necessary, whenever the steps brought them together. Keira thoroughly enjoyed the familiar dance, and her enthusiasm soon convinced Selene and Marcus to join them.

She woke up the next morning with a slight headache and a lot of embarrassment. Thankfully she felt much better after a hearty breakfast of eggs and ham. Keira helped saddle the horses this time, watching the stable boy work.

"The horses love you," she informed him when he carried a feeding bag of oats over to Mini.

He shrugged. "I like horses. I'm sure they can tell."

"No, really." She met his eyes and let hers show silver. "My horse loves you."

"She tell you that, Mistress?" He asked, taking a hasty step back.

"Yes, actually." Keira smiled apologetically. "Don't worry about me kid — I approve of you."

"Sorry Mistress. The last mage we had come through here weren't very friendly."

"I'm sorry to hear that."

He shrugged. "No real harm done, but I wouldn't want on your bad side. You let me know if you or your friends need anything."

Keira ran a hand down Mini's glossy neck. "You did a good job with the horses. That's a great plenty. How long ago did this grumpy mage come through?"

"Eight days, Mistress. And, as much as I don't like to contradict you...grumpy is the wrong word. He was terrifying."

"Was he headed to Polaris?"

The stable boy gave a sharp shake of his head. "He headed straight west."

"Thank you." Keira smiled down at him, then led Mini to wait in the courtyard for the rest of the group.

When they had set off, she told them about the ArKen who had frightened the stable boy, but nobody else seemed interested in pursuing him.

"It doesn't take much to leave a young boy frightened of an ArKen," Selene pointed out, her voice gentle. "You aren't used to it yet, but many people are unsettled by us, even without any encouragement."

"He seemed more than unsettled," Keira insisted as they rode under the forest canopy. "For all we know, that ArKen could be the one who sent the sickness."

Selene shook her head. "For all we know, he isn't."

"Did the boy give you any other details?" Fionn asked.

"No." Keira shook her head. "He wouldn't tell me anything really."

"It may have been merely a bit of showmanship from someone having a bad day. Even if it was a criminal ArKen, we have no way of knowing that it was our culprit," Marcus said in his gravelly voice.

Declan nodded. "I think we have to continue toward Polaris. We don't have enough information to warrant changing course. If we were wrong...."

Keira shuddered at the implication. "What if we go back and question him?"

"It would cost us half a day," Liam pointed out.

The discussion continued in this way until Keira was half convinced that she was overreacting. Fionn was the only one who wanted to follow her instinct, but he was outvoted. Keira had to bow to their greater experience; she let the matter drop.

* * *

Their group followed an old road northwest through the forest. The trees there reached their knobbly branches impossibly far into the sky. Something about them felt ancient, almost aware. In a few places, close to Oaklyra, they were clearly cultivated. In those areas the trees were younger. Keira preferred the ancient oaks and sycamores. She could feel a tremendous strength in them. She wondered if it was magic or just the energy of a plant living, but Declan was too far away to ask, and she didn't want the others to give her another of those *looks*.

They stopped twice to water the horses and relieve themselves. Everyone was nervous and preferred to keep moving, so they ate lunch in the saddle. Keira was the only member of the party perfectly at ease in the forest. She enjoyed letting her awareness unfurl around them and focus in on tiny creatures rummaging for food. Once or twice, she directed a squirrel to a very fine nut close at hand. It was oddly fulfilling and put her in a cheerful mood.

"Do you know you're humming?" Fionn asked in a stage whisper.

"No...I hadn't realized."

"What put you in such a good mood?" He asked, dark hazel eyes meeting her own.

When she told him about her squirrel friends, he laughed out loud. He laughed so hard that his whole body shook. If anyone else had laughed at her like that it would have hurt, but somehow his laughter made her join in.

"This is why I love you," he said, urging his horse forward to chat with Declan.

Keira stared at her hands. *Did he just say what I think he did?* The words sounded so casual, but she couldn't look at him. Her face felt hot. She glanced up surreptitiously, but he wasn't looking at her. He was laughing at something Declan said. She loved his laugh. Keira smiled even as her face burned. *Of course, he only meant that he loves me as a friend.*

When her cheeks had cooled, she reached down to pat Mini's white neck and noticed she was tense. Sending her mind out, Keira found that all of the horses were tense — and the small creatures had stopped their foraging.

Danger! She whispered silently to the others. The ArKen among them looked back at her, and she held a finger to her lips, then pointed upward. An enormous creature was flying in great circles above them. Keira wasn't sure if it had actually spotted them and was afraid to touch its mind. It radiated power. This was a creature of magic, but too small to be a dragon.

Keira tried to drop her mind over the horses, like a blindfold on a narrow bridge. She met with limited success, but managed to lead them slowly and relatively quietly off the road. Liam had communicated to the guards via hand signals what was happening so that nobody fought the horses. Then she dismounted, along with the other travelers, and they gathered in a tight knot.

"What is it?" Marcus hissed, joining them.

"A griffin." Selene whispered through pale lips.

"Did it see us?" Fionn asked.

"I don't think so," Declan replied. "If it had, we'd be dead."

"I thought griffins were thinking beasts?" Keira asked, then lost all semblance of calm as the massive creature landed with a thud.

It lost its feet a moment later, falling to its knees. Keira still trembled with the force of its landing as she looked at the griffin. It was at *least* twice as big as a draft horse, with great wings that seemed too large to belong to a creature its size. Most alarming were its curved beak, dark talons, and cruel eyes.

As a creature of magic, the griffin knew they were there. It had been foolish to hope otherwise. Keira had not touched its mind, but it reached out and touched hers, gold eyes meeting her silver.

"Are you the one that tore me from the sky?" It asked in a voice that was almost unrecognizable as speech.

Keira wasn't sure if it spoke aloud at first because its words seemed to echo in her mind as well. It held no anger, but it did accuse. And its voice was so powerful, she felt sure that it could tear her mind apart if it wanted to.

"You, Silver Maiden are the only one here strong enough. Come out, I won't hurt you."

Keira took a step forward, and Fionn's hand closed on her arm like a vice grip.

"Don't." He whispered urgently.

"You can't lie with your mind."

"It's talking to you?"

Keira nodded.

"*You* can't lie with your mind, but I'd wager that thing can."

"Let go." Keira insisted.

He removed his hand, and she clambered out of the thicket and onto the road. There was no discussing it with the others, and she heard several of the guards call out in surprise. Glancing over her shoulder, Keira saw that the other ArKen looked ready to attack. The magic-less guards among them held their spears at the ready.

Keira turned back to the griffin. It was unwise to look away. Instead, she strode directly in front of it and curtsied deeply. It flicked its lion's tail and licked a talon, looking like nothing so much as an overlarge house cat. Keira sat on her knees in the dirt, facing it. Dry wagon ruts cut through the road on either side of her. She tried to sit straight, mimicking the griffin's posture.

"*Did you drag me to the Earth, child?*" It asked in a voice that was half purr, half clicking beak.

She shook her head. "I would not dare to do such a thing, even if it was within my power."

"*I felt you exploring the sky.*" Its eyes flashed golden and Keira felt her silver show.

"I withdrew as soon as I felt your presence."

"*Wise little thing, aren't you?*"

Keira felt a great pressure on her mind and nearly tipped over.

"*If not you, then who?*" This time there was anger.

"*It wasn't me!*" Keira gasped, her mental voice far louder than her breathless assertion.

The griffin winced, but flicked its ears with renewed curiosity. "*Why are you here, in this forest that should be mine?*"

"We have come to treat an illness."

"*Ah.*" It flicked its tail. "*In that case you are heading in the wrong direction. The source of this pestilence lies west of here. Else I would not be crossing a human road.*"

"You landed hard, are you all right?"

The griffin chortled. "*Why should it matter to you, human girl. Your silver is strong, but you are not connected to this land as I am.*"

Keira thought she understood what he meant. "Perhaps this illness is what made you fall?"

He ruffled his feathers, and his eyes flashed, making Keira wince. "*Perhaps. If you give me a push, I should be able to fly again. And as payment, I will not eat you, or your little friends.*"

Keira shivered. "And what of the next humans you meet?"

"*There will be no next humans. I keep to myself.*"

"Even when you're bored?" A brave guard had joined Keira in the road.

Keira turned to see that it was Marcus. The grizzled old

soldier wore a serious expression. Keira thought the griffin would strike him down.

Instead, it laughed. *"Even when I'm bored."*

Keira had a sudden image of the griffin swooping in and out over waves on a crystal clear lake.

If you are going to help me, I have to trust you not to burn my mind. Can I do that?

It was not spoken aloud, but Keira nodded. She could never have hurt this creature.

She stood and approached him, reaching one shaking hand out to touch his massive beak. Her heart pounded. Unfurling her mind, she found that the golden fire of the creature was wrapped in a web of darkness, almost like a net. It turned her stomach to look at the darkness. It took all her strength and concentration, but she burned it away. *Very carefully.*

It was the most demanding use of magic she had ever attempted. When she finished, Keira collapsed in the dirt. She shivered uncontrollably as a blanket of frost spread across the ground. The griffin stood, made a sweeping bow to his rescuer, and sent her an impression. With two beats of his enormous wings, the griffin leaped into the air.

Obeying his directions, Keira placed both her hands on the ground and drew a little heat from somewhere deep under the dirt. She never would have found it without his help, or even known how to use it, but she was certain that it saved her life.

Before she found the strength to get to her feet, she found herself in Fionn's arms. It was delightfully warm, and she didn't argue or pull away as he lifted her to her feet

"What happened?"

As the group moved back into the road, eyes still on the sky, Keira explained as best she could. The ArKen among them already had a fair idea of what happened, but they understood better as Keira supplemented her speech with images.

"We *have* to go west." Keira concluded.

"I'm not going to trust the word of a griffin," Liam said flatly. "I'm going to Polaris."

"But all the legends say they never lie," Keira spluttered.

Declan shook his head as well. "In either case, I'd be useless against whoever caused this illness. In Polaris, at least my skills will be of use."

"Are you suggesting we split up?' Fionn asked in alarm.

"I think so." Declan paused. "I hate the idea, but it may save lives."

"I think it's a good idea." Keira agreed. "A smaller group is more likely to find this ArKen anyway."

After a quarter of an hour of arguing, the party finally came to an agreement. Declan, Liam, and most of the guards would continue on to Polaris and treat the victims to the best of their abilities. Keira worried they would just fall ill themselves, but the guards promised to get the others out if they showed any symptoms. Keira, Fionn, Selene, and Marcus would head west, cutting straight through the forest in the direction the griffin had indicated. Their party was smaller because the magic-less soldiers would be more useful dispensing medicine than trying to fight a powerful ArKen.

"Be careful." Declan urged.

"We will. Don't worry about us, Master Declan." Keira said brightly as a knot of tension formed in her stomach.

She hugged Mini tightly before turning and walking into the woods. *Be good*, she whispered in the confused horse's mind, along with a comforting image of her returning. Hurricane looked just as baffled as his master charged into the thick underbrush. Each of their smaller party carried a heavy pack with the bare essentials. How strange that Keira was choosing a possible fight over the chance to heal. But she could feel it in her bones — this was the victims' only chance.

Fifteen

Walking through the forest was exhausting. Keira's boots were soon caked in layers of squelching mud, as were the six inches of skirt above her hem. All four of them were covered in scratches from head to toe in under an hour. The forest might not be as sunny, but it was muggy, and early mosquitoes buzzed menacingly before drinking their fill from the hapless travelers.

It was only a few hours before night fell and the four of them gathered around a small fire. Keira and Selene explored the area around the camp with their magical senses, but other than a few small animals, they were alone. Marcus built the fire and Fionn gathered wood while the two women rolled out everyone's sleeping bags and got dinner started.

A cool wind parted the trees above them, but there were no stars to be seen, only dark clouds. Keira sighed in disappointment, then felt the first drops of what would prove to be a dreadful storm. Keira had always thought that she liked thunderstorms, but that night, she learned that she hated them. She liked the sound of rain, particularly if she was safely tucked away indoors. She *didn't* like the hair-raising feeling of lightning striking close by, or the howl of an angry wind.

They took turns at watch that night, but nobody got much sleep. The wind was loud enough to wake a sleeping dragon, and the rain cut across them in painful sheets. In the morning, when the rain finally died down, Keira might have cried from relief if she wasn't so dog tired. Whatever she had done for the griffin still pulled at her limbs. Keira had really needed the night's rest.

"Are we planning to get moving right away?" She asked, covering her mouth with one hand while she yawned and stretched.

"I think we should," Marcus said tiredly.

He was sitting by an obviously failed attempt at a fire, but nonetheless eating a bowl of steaming beans. Keira looked around and found a pot of them sitting at Selene's feet.

"You cooked breakfast?" Keira asked. "Thank you."

"I thought we could all use something hot." Selene rested her head on her knees as she ate, seemingly oblivious to the mud that coated her legs.

Fionn brought Keira a heaping bowl of beans and a clay mug filled with a black liquid. It smelled good but tasted awful. She spit it out.

"What *is* this?" She spluttered.

"Coffee. I thought we could use it." Fionn said, grinning at her reaction. "It's a delicacy, *imported*."

It was so much worse than the coffee that Declan had tried to give her that Keira hadn't even recognized it. She groaned.

Marcus laughed heartily, "I've never understood why the nobility insist on calling anything expensive a delicacy. I will stick to my good old tea. Thank you *very* much."

"Some people prefer it with milk and sugar. We don't have either with us." Fionn shrugged. "You don't have to drink it."

Keira took another experimental sip. It was awful and coated her mouth and throat in a way that made her teeth feel grimy.

"I don't think it's for me, but thank you for sharing."

He shrugged and reclaimed her mug, taking a long drink. "I'll be awake while you all fall asleep in the saddle."

Selene shrugged. "Protein is better than caffeine, besides tea does have some."

She passed Keira a cold cup with leaves and yawned, "I'm a bit tired, if you don't mind."

Keira heated their teacups and they continued their breakfast in silence. Nobody really wanted to talk, and Fionn was the only one who seemed to be in a good mood, although Keira suspected his cheerfulness was a mask for nerves. Once she'd had her fill of warm beans, Keira got up and wrapped her bedding in a tight roll, drying it with magic as she went. Instead of heating it, she simply suctioned the water into the air. It was more efficient and felt safer.

She performed the same service for the others. It would do them no good to carry the weight of soaked blankets with them. Looking around, she saw that the bags had miraculously stayed dry. Thank whoever had decided to waterproof them. Everyone's clothing was at least damp however, so she dried them each by turns.

The forest was oddly quiet as they marched through the underbrush. Some instinct told Keira to keep her mind to herself. The most she dared was to check with a passing hawk if it had seen anyone. All it had seen was a rabbit that scurried into a hidey-hole. Apparently, the bird's eye view of the forest was mostly tree-tops. He was headed back to the plains, filled with disappointment.

When they were discussing stopping for lunch, Keira turned to find a crossbow leveled at her face. The man that held it looked like he had been living rough for a while, with torn clothes and dirt-streaked features. Keira held her hands up to show she would cooperate, then looked around to see that the rest of the little group was in a similar predicament. She let her mind slowly drift out and found that there were no magic users among them. Eight bandits had them surrounded.

"Sorry friend, can we help you?" Marcus asked in his gravelly voice.

"We'll take your packs." The man who held the crossbow leveled at Marcus' chest said tightly.

Their little party backed up until they were in a tight knot. The bandits looked worse for wear, their clothing darned repeatedly and shadows pooling under their eyes. Keira wondered what had happened to these men. *Why would they even be in this part of the forest? It doesn't seem like a very profitable location for banditry.*

She slid her pack off. "What happened to you?" She asked softly.

The man who had his attention focused on her shook his head. "Bag."

Keira glanced at Selene, who nodded. With a little effort of concentration all four of the crossbows in their attackers hands burst into flame. There were shouts of surprise as the men dropped them. Just as quickly, Keira put the fire out. She reached down and grabbed the crossbow at her feet, turning it on the bandit before her as her eyes flashed silver.

At the same time, Selene called up a menacing whirlwind. The wind howled as it whipped through the trees, throwing dirt in the newcomer's eyes.

Keira grinned wickedly and reached into their muscles, forcing them to sit in the mud. She heard eight thumps, just as Marcus was drawing his blade. He looked around wildly to see Keira with her hand up and her eyes glowing silver.

She imagined what it looked like from his perspective. She had just used her knowledge of healing to force eight men off their feet. Truth be told, she could have done much worse. Keira thought of the possibilities with sudden horror. With her knowledge of the human body, and her strength in magic, she could send someone into unimaginable agony, cause a fever so high they hallucinated. She could even stop their heart. Keira's own heart raced at the thought, her stomach twisting with sudden nausea.

The grin had faded from her face, to be replaced by wide eyes and a blank stare of horror. *But I didn't do any of those things,* she soothed herself. *I simply used my power to restrain.* She hoped it was a justifiable use. It somehow seemed wrong to turn someone's own body against them.

Wrenching her thoughts back to the moment, Keira let flames lick the crossbow in her hands again. She chose to fuel it with her own energy instead of the wood, and it produced a disconcerting visual effect.

The man in front of her stayed silent. It seemed like he wouldn't have been *able* to speak. He was quite literally quaking in his boots. Keira noted that they were rather fine boots. *A little too fine.* She narrowed her eyes.

"Where did you get those boots?" Marcus asked, preempting her.

He shook his head, mouth moving silently as he watched the heatless fire spread up her arms, singeing nothing.

Selene spoke, "Perhaps a different approach, hon." She placed a hand on Keira's shoulder.

Keira nodded and snuffed the fire. In the sudden dimness, she struggled to see the men in the dirt. "There's rope in my pack."

Marcus and Fionn quickly tied up the would-be bandits. They were surprisingly cooperative, eyeing Keira as they held out their hands to be tied. One man tried to flee, but she dragged him back by the leg as if a giant invisible hand had grasped his ankle. His panicked cries made her wince, but she had never felt so powerful. She *hated* it.

Fionn built a large fire pit and then Selene stacked the wood he carried. Marcus guarded the prisoners carefully. Nobody talked much, but they had decided a good meal and a rest would do them all some good. Keira sorted through their provisions and fetched some water. By the time the smell of stew drifted over their camp, the prisoners had calmed down enough to look longingly at the pot.

"Time to talk." Marcus stood with his arms crossed. "What are you doing out here?"

"We're just simple men, sir. We were hungry so we …"

"Don't lie." Keira said sharply. "I will know."

It was true. She wouldn't have probed around anyone's mind, but just by spreading her senses around them, she could feel basic intentions. This man was full of stories and secrets.

He swallowed hard. "We didn't mean any real harm, honest."

That was true too.

"Answer the question." Fionn said, handing the man a bowl of stew.

"I can't."

"Why?"

"Cause he's a damn fool," another of the bound men said, spitting. "I'll talk."

"So talk," Marcus prompted after a moment of silence.

"We were part of a small unit, stationed in enemy territory. But our commander is ill. Dying, looks like. We thought you'd be our salvation. This far out in the woods? Hoped you'd be herbalists and we'd find some medicine."

"Your commander?" Keira asked.

He nodded. "We don't actually..."

"Shut up!" One of the others kicked him from his place in the dirt.

Keira let her eyes flash silver and he shrank away.

"*Do* go on," she said, as though they were having a conversation at a fancy party and had merely been interrupted by a dance ending.

"We don't actually know her name," he clarified. "She's an ArKen from Ravena."

"And where are you from?" Fionn asked.

"Eimar," he answered, eyes darting away.

"How many are with your leader now?" Marcus asked.

"Only the sick. There are a dozen of them, but...they're mostly bed ridden."

Keira and Fionn shared a look as Fionn pressed a bowl of stew into the last prisoner's hand.

"And your commander is sick as well?" She asked.

"The sickest of the lot. She won't even let us touch her. She claims she's dying." His voice cracked on the last word.

Keira could have sworn the man was close to tears, but if he was, he managed to control himself. She accepted a bowl from Fionn, then sat down to eat her stew. "If you lead us to your camp, it's possible we could help her."

"Don't you dare, you *yellow-bellied* traitor!" One of the others yelled, spilling his meal as he tried to attack his comrade.

"I'll do it." The cooperative one agreed, ignoring his companion.

Keira thought he was just attached to this commander of his, and desperate. But the easy cooperation was disconcerting. It felt too much like a trap. The party discussed it for an hour, at length, finally deciding to take a short nap and then send Keira and Fionn to investigate. The hope was that arriving in the dead of night would provide them an element of surprise and a chance to go unnoticed if the others' conditions had been exaggerated.

Fionn refused to untie their guide. Instead, he walked in front of them, hands tied in front of him and a rope trailing back to Fionn's hand. Keira felt the precaution a little unnecessary, but Fionn couldn't feel how worried the man was for his fellows.

"How far is it?" She whispered.

"I don't know." The cooperative bandit glanced up, but couldn't see the stars because of the clouds. "We walked at least an hour, but everything looks different during the day."

Keira sighed in frustration but took a deep breath to center herself. She focused on placing her feet quietly. Fionn reached his free hand out and rubbed her back. His touch left a trail of goose bumps and Keira smiled, glad of the darkness. Cautiously, she reached out to night creatures around them to help navigate the shadowed night.

The smallest creatures ran from her touch. Something had them spooked. Looking around, Keira found a great horned owl. It wasn't interested in helping her but didn't object to sharing what it knew. The humans were near. It was annoyed because their scent had sent the small things into hiding. Poor thing was hungry.

Keira put a hand to her lips and crept ahead of the others. Fionn followed her lead, holding their prisoner back with a hand on his shoulder. It didn't take much; he was still being cooperative. Keira found a small clearing ahead. A few trees had been cut down to broaden it, but it was still small.

As they stepped into the camp, they discovered a handful of bodies littering the ground, scattered around a bed of soft embers. Keira cautiously examined them with her magical senses and found that they weren't breathing. Moving through the camp with painful slowness, she found four people alive. One of them was clearly the leader. She rested on a blanket and took rattling breaths. Sending her mind into the bodies of the dead, Keira found that none of them were recent enough to be resuscitated.

"I'm sorry." She whispered, placing a gentle hand on their captive's shoulder.

"What?" He looked panicked.

"Most of them are gone. I'll do what I can for those who live."

"Is she?" He grabbed the front of Keira's dress with his bound hands, like a man clinging to a root in a cliff wall.

Fionn ripped him off her with a growl.

Keira shook her head. "She yet lives."

"Treat her first. Please."

"She'll be fine for a few minutes." Keira said, more confident than she felt.

One of the others was clinging to life by a thread. Keira knelt by his side, placing a careful hand on his forehead. Closing her eyes, she sent her awareness into his body. It was terrifying. She was momentarily overwhelmed by all the sensations from her dream.

Fire raged in his muscles, and his lungs crackled, but she could not find the source of the illness. She cooled the fire, and did her best to relieve the damage to his lungs. He breathed easier, and she knew he could hold on for a little while. When she opened her eyes, for the briefest moment she thought she saw a series of black threads spider-webbing over his prone form. She yanked her hand back.

Looking very carefully at her own hands with both her eyes and her magic, she saw that one thin line of the black fire snaked up her arm. Keira knelt again, placing a hand on the damp earth, and drew from its central fire to burn away the invading energy.

"This is bad," she said to Fionn. "I don't understand what she's done, but this ArKen is the source of the illness."

"Is there anything you can do?"

"Maybe."

"Be careful."

She nodded and approached the dying ArKen, kneeling beside her.

"Don't......touch.....me...." The woman breathed, each word punctuated by a ragged breath.

"Maybe I can help you."

"You....can't."

What did you do? Keira asked, both with her voice and her mind.

The woman recoiled from her mental touch, throwing up shields the likes of which Keira had never seen. Everything was covered in the black spiderwebs. Her breath came in rasping gasps.

"I understand that you don't want to hurt me. You have something contagious, but I can't help if you don't talk to me."

"You....can't....help....." She struggled for breath to speak.

Keira's eyes flashed silver. "What if I can?"

I did something terrible, came the mental reply.

"What was it?" Keira prompted gently.

I attempted magic I didn't understand. It was meant to sever the magic of ArKen. But....I didn't understand what that meant, the woman sent, tears streaking down her cheeks.

Keira nodded. "It affected a griffin. That was unexpected. Will you let me examine these dark threads?"

The woman nodded. It looked exhausting.

Keira closed her eyes and opened her mind. *If this woman didn't understand what severing another's magic would mean, she must not be a Natural ArKen. Of course it would kill.* What Keira didn't understand was how it spread. She followed the traces of burning darkness that snaked over and through this woman. They flowed into the air and northward, but where did they come from?

Her eyes flew open. It was *her*. This woman had corrupted her very essence into a darkness that would consume everyone. Keira breathed quickly, her heart pounding at the horror of this corruption. She gagged and nearly threw up. When she had her stomach under control, Fionn pulled her in for a tight hug. Keira relaxed into his warmth and cried. She was right, Keira probably couldn't help.

Their guide ignored the woman's protests and cradled her in his still-bound arms. "Can you help her?"

Keira shook her head. "I doubt it, but I have to do something. She's killing everyone. It was meant to affect ArKen, but she didn't realize that everyone has magic."

Fionn stood in open-mouthed horror. He spent enough time with Declan and Keira to understand the implications. Keira watched the threads of darkness burn up the distraught man's arms.

"I *will* try, but you have to put her down."

He nodded and moved back. Keira saw the darkness slow, but it was still eating away at him. He'd be dead before a day passed if nothing were done. Unfortunately, Keira could not spare the energy if she were going to make a real attempt to stop this at the source. She'd have to hope she could heal him afterward.

"Listen." She whispered to Fionn. "If….if this doesn't work, you have to kill her. And probably me. Or everyone will die. *Everyone*, you understand."

"I can't."

Keira shrugged and set to work. Looking down at her own

hands, she saw the nasty web of darkness had taken root. She burned it away, then touched the corrupted ArKen's face with one hand. Keira closed her eyes and buried her other hand in the dirt, comforted by the heat at its heart.

Then she set to work. She felt herself grow cold as she used her own fire to burn away some of the cobwebs. It was no good. Even as she destroyed them, they snaked through. It was the nature of this woman's magic now.

Keira considered, *perhaps I'm approaching this the wrong way?*

She poured healing magic into the physical side of the malady. The woman breathed easier, but the darkness persisted, spreading through the air like a dark aurora. Keira sighed and backed off, burning away the darkness that was wrapping itself around her so that she could think in peace.

She examined the nature of her own magic. *Why does it appear light?* It was her life force, she knew that much. And it connected her to the world in a way that most were not. That was the benefit of being a Natural. She could draw on strength that was not her own, tied into threads of power that snaked through the world.

Sudden understanding burned through her mind. *This woman artificially created that connection!* She looked up, with that magic sense, and realized that the dark aurora was simply one such thread of the innumerable that she could always feel.

With that knowledge, the answer was simple. Keira reached out to the thread and instead of trying to burn it away, she transferred some of the life from the others into the dying limb. It worked. *Very* slowly, the darkness faded to light. The source of the corruption was a connection that was never meant to be.

Keira turned to the woman, grabbed her by the shoulders, and met her eyes. "This is going to hurt. *A lot.*"

She nodded.

Keira tore the threads of the world from the woman, sealing the last of the corruption with a little of her own power before letting them return to their natural flow. The woman screamed uncontrollably as she worked. Keira couldn't blame her. Their guide tried to tackle Keira, but Fionn restrained him.

Keira ignored them both and focused on her work. She peeled away the woman's shielding. It would do her no good. It was a natural defense against a connection she was never meant to harness, but it locked it in place. When she had finished, the woman lay panting through a hoarse throat. She was the only one affected by the corruption now, though the physical damage to the others would have to be healed.

Shaking with cold, Keira knelt and reached into the earth, trying to patch the frayed web of connections that had been poisoned. She had, by necessity, severed a few. Keira could feel that warmth filled her entire eyes instead of the iris as it did when her silver showed. Her muscles shook. Her mind nearly fled, but Fionn's gentle touch on her back steadied her.

Shivering and exhausted, Keira collapsed in the dirt. She had been at least partially successful, but she had no way to know how extensive the damage to the web of life was. While she knew she had no choice, the unknown consequences would haunt her. She wept as she drifted into oblivion.

Sixteen

When she awoke, Keira was wrapped in a blanket near a toasty fire. She was far enough away not to have to worry about sparks, but the blaze warmed her exposed face and hands, relieving the cold. She smiled, and nearly drifted back to sleep before remembering. Instead, she sat bolt upright — a mistake, given the way her muscles screamed at her — and looked around in confusion.

After a moment of panic, she realized she was back at their camp. The would-be bandits were all tied up, with the exception of the ill. Six figures were laid out on blankets. None of them moved much, but each was breathing steadily.

"What happened?" Keira asked Marcus, who was keeping a night watch.

"You slept for a day and a half. I don't know much, but Fionn said you worked some powerful magic," he explained, voice soft in the darkness.

Keira cupped a hand on her forehead. "I guess I didn't really have time to explain."

Selene dozed beside her, but Fionn was out of sight.

"He went to get help." Marcus explained when he saw her looking around.

She nodded. "Have they been healed?"

Marcus shook his head. "Selene is no healer, but they've all had medicine for the fever. Best we could do."

Keira nodded and wiggled out of her blanket. "I'll get to work then."

"Take care of yourself first, kiddo. Water. Food."

She thought about it and nodded. Getting unsteadily to her feet, she asked, "Privy?"

Marcus pointed, and Keira went to relieve herself. Her legs were rubbery as she moved around camp, taking care of the necessary pieces of self-care one apparently missed during a thirty-six hour nap. After she had something in her stomach, Keira felt much better.

She crept to the nearest of the sick and placed a hand on their forehead. Closing her eyes, she burned away the last traces of darkness that still clung to the man's chest. This time, she didn't use her own fire, instead pulling from the earth. She did what she could to reverse the damage to his lungs, and reversed the injury inflammation had done to his muscles. Then she crept to each of the others and performed the same office.

When she finished with the last of the men, she knelt beside the woman who had been the source of this calamity. Keira cried as she tried to heal her. She managed to ease her breathing, but her muscles were a hopeless case. Keira focused intently on the muscles that the ArKen needed to breath. She poured some of her own strength into her, but it was useless.

Whatever she had done to the threads of the world had corrupted her own energy in a way that was permanent and made magical healing ineffective. Keira turned red rimmed eyes on the man who had so worried for this woman. She shook her head.

"No," he gasped. "No!"

He crawled to her side and held her in his arms, crying harder than Keira had ever seen a man cry. It was startling, and she got to her feet and backed away. She felt like she was witnessing something that should be private. She had at least made it safe for them to say their goodbyes.

"Who is she?" Keira asked one of the other men.

"Countess Le Brouch." Marcus answered quietly, white-knuckled hand gripping his polearm.

"Countess....?" Keira looked back at her, "The Queen's cousin? The one who eloped?"

He nodded. Keira stood beside him and watched her die. Reluctantly, she helped tie up the recently healed prisoners. The only one that remained untied was the man lost to grief. He did not move, and Keira left Marcus to watch him while she got some sleep. Magical exhaustion still pulled at her, body and mind.

* * *

Keira stood against one wall of the throne room with Declan. After the king and queen had been briefed on their separate adventures, she had been invited in as a lie detector. Keira wasn't thrilled with her role. Now that she'd had time to reflect, she had qualms about this use of magic. Besides, leaving her mind open to the soldier's emotions, all she felt was grief. Harlan had loved the countess deeply. His grief left little room for deception.

"Why did my cousin do this?" Queen Olivia asked of the man in chains.

Her grief spilled into Keira's mind as well, since she didn't know how to open herself to only one person at a time. Silent, sympathetic tears slipped down Keira's cheeks.

"Our king promised her the ruling of this province, once we had conquered it."

"But...." The queen stammered from her throne.

King Herbert put an arm around his wife and Keira had to throw up mental shields at the force of the grief that tore through Harlan's chest. Her shields were thin, and Keira had to put her hand over her mouth to stifle her own sobs.

"Genevieve expected to be chosen as queen. Is it any surprise she never got over the shock when her poor country cousin was chosen instead?" Harlan asked.

"But she didn't even know me!" King Herbert exclaimed.

"Gen always valued her title, but I didn't think she was capable of murder," Queen Olivia murmured, almost to herself.

"She wasn't!" Her mourner declared hotly.

The king glanced at Keira. She nodded to show he was telling the truth.

"Explain," he growled.

"She didn't murder anyone. She was the victim of this curse as much as anyone." His voice cracked.

"Your Majesties, perhaps it would be best if my apprentice explained?" Declan offered.

"Can you?" King Herbert asked.

Keira could not get used to being so casually addressed by this bear of a King. She curtsied on shaky legs. "I believe I can clarify, Sire."

He motioned her forward, and Keira stumbled to obey, coming to a halt beside the prisoner.

"What does he mean?"

"The countess...she was not a murderer. She just didn't understand the implications of the magic she attempted, Your Majesty."

"And what did she attempt?" Queen Olivia asked, her voice gentle.

"She thought that Eimar would have a greater chance of victory if Ravena had no ArKen. But...she didn't understand the nature of magic. Magic is the force of life itself. To separate an ArKen from their magic means death. And everyone has magic, not just practicing ArKen. This is why her corruption...the illness...spread."

The royal couple exchanged a communicative glance. "Go on," King Herbert rumbled.

"Well, essentially she corrupted her life force and, because she artificially connected herself with the world threads, it corrupted the creatures and the land around her."

"World threads?" The queen asked, puzzled.

"It...isn't the technical term. I'm afraid I don't know what they're called. I'm still learning to wield my magic. But, it is....the way I think of the instinctive connections that Natural ArKen feel. Not everyone is meant to have so much magic pass through them. She was doomed the moment she created a connection she wasn't born to bear."

Queen Olivia bowed her head, grieving the cousin she had grown up with. Keira understood, and shielded her mind to allow her some privacy. Even if a family member betrayed you, that love would never leave.

"What's going to happen to us?" The bound man asked after a long silence.

"For now, you are prisoners of war, but your king has already been contacted to discuss a peace treaty. Ravena has never been a vengeful nation."

Keira was caught unaware by a wave of fear from the man. It was so intense it broke through her flimsy shields. She had only learned the technique from watching Le Brouch and this was her first practice, after all.

"He's afraid." She blurted immediately, alerting her own king to what the enemy combatant so skillfully concealed.

"Why?"

"I don't know, Your Majesty. But it's intense."

"I fear for my king," he said bitingly. "He cannot come here."

"Is that accurate, Apprentice Smith?"

Keira nodded. "I believe so, Your Majesty."

"Why can he not come?" The queen asked, voice nearly as soft as when she had addressed Keira.

Keira felt another wave of grief. The man had lost so much, and he feared losing more. He remained silent, and Keira suspected it was to hide his weakness.

"He's afraid for his king's safety. If he's harmed during negotiations it will be his fault because he's the one that led us to the countess," Keira explained for him.

"King Duncan will be perfectly safe here," King Herbert exclaimed, visibly shocked at the insinuation.

"Of course he will. What do you take us for?" The queen added.

"The neighbors who hoard their wealth while we starve," he said bitterly.

The royal couple exchanged another pregnant look. The prisoner was dismissed, and Declan was called forward to stand beside his pupil. The few guards in the room relaxed as the foreign soldier left. They seemed to regard Master Declan Elers and his pupil as loyal and safe, even if they were ArKen. Keira noticed that two of the guards had a silver stripe on the arms of their uniforms, although neither had been part of their traveling party.

"So, Master Elers, when will your apprentice be joining the ranks of our battlemages?" The king asked Declan.

Keira stared in open-mouthed horror, the world tilting around her.

"I believe she is nearly ready to leave my tutelage, Your Majesty. Keira has firm control of her magic. The only thing she lacks is scientific knowledge, something I believe she has the curiosity and motivation to pursue on her own, with limited guidance."

"Scientific knowledge?" The queen asked.

Declan nodded. "Yes, Highness. Keira desires nothing more than to be a healer."

"But she defeated the enemy ArKen!" King Herbert boomed, laughing.

Keira stepped forward and curtsied low.

"You have something to add, Apprentice Smith?" The queen asked.

She struggled to keep her voice steady as she spoke. "Your Majesties, I didn't defeat anyone. There *was* no battle. My great accomplishment was one of healing. I repaired most of the magical damage, and I healed the surviving victims."

"Is Master Elers correct in his statement of your wishes?" Queen Olivia asked, her eyes crinkling kindly.

"Yes, Your Highness. I would prefer to use my magic for healing, rather than battle."

King Herbert laughed at his young subject, a deep laugh that made his belly shake. "So you shall. When will your apprentice be ready to serve as a healer?"

"She is ready with supervision now. But to fully train her as a healer will take at least two more years of study, more likely three."

"Very well. Miss Smith, I hope you can swallow your pride and continue to study under a lowly Seeker."

"Master Elers is a wonderful teacher," Keira rebuffed.

"I believe she would greatly benefit from studying at the university," Elers hedged. "The magic Keira worked in that forest is well beyond my understanding."

The king frowned. "You think her admission necessary?"

"I think it advisable. Keira's gift is strong, one of the strongest this kingdom has ever seen. With the type of magic that she's capable of wielding, it would be best for her to undergo more advanced training, with a wider focus than just healing."

Keira's jaw dropped.

"I don't mean to imply that she should serve as a battlemage," Declan hurried to add. "Quite the contrary. I believe that would be a true blunder."

King Herbert folded his hands, his eyebrows drawing down. "We will consider your advice. You are both dismissed. Apprentice Smith, thank you for your service to this kingdom and its people.

Keira curtsied deeply. "It would not have been possible without your gracious gift of education and most excellent library."

"Herbert is quite the curator," the queen agreed, smiling

warmly at her husband as the two ArKen were ushered into the corridor.

As soon as they made it into the hall, Keira leaned against the wall with a shaky laugh. She could feel her magic, humming softly below the surface. Her future might be unsettled, but instead of the anxiety her magic had induced a year earlier, she felt comforted. Apprentice Keira Smith, a future Mistress of magic straightened her spine. Despite all they had been through, she saw a future filled with joy.

Author Newsletter

I hope that you enjoyed Showing Silver, Book One of The ArKen Duology. If you would like to receive an email with updates on the sequel, you can join my newsletter using the QR code below

Evelyn Linwood's Newsletter

Acknowledgments

This book has been burning in my brain for half my life. So, I have to thank the two discord servers full of writers who helped me get started. You helped me move from the vague wish to be an author "someday" to holding a finished book in my hands.

I'd also like to thank my wonderful, supportive husband. Without you, writing would be a different, far lonelier experience.

I'd like to thank my mom, for alpha reading and helping with proofreading. And my dad, for blindly assuming I must be a good writer, even if he hasn't read my work (He mostly reads nonfiction). Your support has been invaluable.

Lastly, I want to thank my map maker (William Bauer) and cover designer (Yosbe Designs). Both turned out beautifully and I am thrilled to have them represent this work.

About the Author

Evelyn is an enthusiastic Fantasy writer from Michigan. She always dreamed of publishing "someday". She started writing in middle school for her own enjoyment, but began writing in earnest in December of 2019. Since then, she has made connections with other writers and found a support structure that helps her creativity flourish.

When she isn't writing, Evelyn spends most of her time with her husband, their cat Sammy, and their dog Nova. She refills her creative well by reading, gaming, listening to music, and playing with yarn.

Made in the USA
Monee, IL
27 August 2025

24384786R00135